FOUCAULT IN WARSAW

First edition, 2021
All rights reserved

Library of Congress Cataloging-in-Publication Data: Available.
ISBN-13: 978-1-948830-36-2 | ISBN-10: 1-948830-36-1

This project is supported in part the New York State Council on the Arts with the support of Governor Andrew M. Cuomo and the New York State Legislature.

NEW YORK STATE OF OPPORTUNITY. | Council on the Arts

This publication has been supported by the ©POLAND Translation Program.

BOOK INSTITUTE
©POLAND

Printed on acid-free paper in the United States of America.

Cover Design by Daniel Benneworth-Gray
Interior Design by Anthony Blake

Open Letter is the University of Rochester's nonprofit, literary translation press:
Dewey Hall 1-219, Box 278968, Rochester, NY 14627

www.openletterbooks.org

FOUCAULT IN WARSAW

REMIGIUSZ RYZIŃSKI

Translated from the Polish by Sean Gasper Bye

OPEN LETTER
LITERARY TRANSLATIONS FROM THE UNIVERSITY OF ROCHESTER

In the stubborn, bright sun of Polish liberty.

History of Madness

THE HERO OF THIS BOOK IS MICHEL FOUCAULT.

But not only him. It's Warsaw, too.

And also the boys whose company Foucault enjoyed most.

The linguistic gender mixing—"girls," "sisters," "her"—comes from the subcultural slang that these men often use to address one another, and to speak about themselves.

"Husband" refers to a homosexual partner. And "straight" means a heterosexual man, whom at times one might desire.

1

URBAN LEGEND

Michel Foucault came to Poland in October 1958.

He took a position as the first director of the newly-founded Center for French Culture at the University of Warsaw.

It was in Warsaw that he finished his doctoral thesis, later published as *History of Madness*.

Yet in mid-1959, he was forced to leave Poland.

The reason was a certain boy.

Jurek.

No one ever figured out who this boy really was.

IN SEARCH OF MICHEL FOUCAULT

The Institute of National Remembrance was the first place I turned to when seeking traces of Michel Foucault in Poland.

I was not the first to look at the Institute (commonly known by its Polish acronym IPN). Others had made repeated attempts to locate information about Foucault. It went without saying that the first director of the Center for French Culture in communist-era Warsaw would have been under surveillance.

There were definitely files on him.

The IPN: "In response to your Application for access to documents for the purpose of conducting academic research, submitted as per art. 36, sec. 1, pt. 2 of the Institute of National Remembrance/Commission for the Prosecution of Crimes Against the Polish Nation Act of December 18, 1998 (Journal of Laws 2007, No. 63, item 424 [amended]), we hereby inform you that a preliminary survey of materials regarding Michel Foucault, b. 10/15/1926, conducted for the query titled: *Michel Foucault in Warsaw (1958–1959)*, has returned no results. The Divisional Office for the Access and Archiving of IPN Documents in Warsaw has concluded its execution of this application."

I realized the lack of information at the IPN didn't mean that there was none, but rather it hadn't been discovered yet. So I wrote out the appropriate applications and started searching for Michel Foucault on my own.

Everywhere I turned, I got the same result.

The University of Warsaw's documentation has no information about Michel Foucault's time at the philosophy department from 1958 to 1959.

Nor did I have any luck with my searches at the Jagiellonian University in Kraków or the University of Gdańsk, where, according to biographical information, Foucault guest-lectured. There was nothing at the Polish Academy of Sciences. A survey of files in the University of Warsaw's philosophy department and the Institute of Romance Languages from later years also turned up nothing.

At the Center for French Culture, Foucault's archives were unavailable. The Institut Français in Warsaw and Kraków knew nothing, except that Foucault had, in fact, been in Poland. The French Embassy sent general information about French–Polish cooperation from that period, but there was no mention at all of Foucault.

There are no archives from Orbis, the government travel agency that might have had information about the Hotel Bristol where Foucault's biographical records say he lived for some time. In the Okęcie Airport archives, there is no data on Foucault's possible flights. Museums, cultural institutions, the Polish Press Agency, the magazines *Życie Warszawy* and *Przekrój*, and the Palace of Culture and Science have no information. Nor are there any records at the Auschwitz-Birkenau State Museum or at the famous psychiatric hospital in Tworki.

The archives of the Capital City of Warsaw and the Museum of Literature contain no trace of the name Foucault.

There seemed to be no witnesses to his time here.

No memoirs, letters, documents, not a single photograph.

Michel Foucault's time in Poland seemed to be the stuff of legends.

THE RIGHT CATALOGUE NUMBER

I searched for information about Michel Foucault for over a year.

I went back to the Institute of National Remembrance many times.

Hundreds of musty-smelling files.

Papers, notes, photos, reports, denunciations, classified information, instructions and orders, conversation transcripts, and secret collaborators' observations.

Keywords: necrophilia, pathology, fetish.

Dirty hands.

Dust.

Stickiness.

Obsession.

I looked through the archives from every possible angle. I pored through catalogues, exhausting the search engines with different combinations of queries and synonyms. No one knew what the key was. So I typed in:

Michel Foucault

just Foucault

just Michel

Paul Foucault (which was his real name).

Nothing.

I started looking for information in the files of people I suspected knew Foucault.

I searched people connected with France, embassy employees, people from the cultural world, artists.

I looked through the archives of prominent novelists, poets, and critics from that era: Jerzy Andrzejewski, Jarosław Iwaszkiewicz, Tadeusz Kotarbiński, Miron Białoszewski, Zygmunt Mycielski, Paweł Hertz, Jerzy Waldorff, Edward Stachura, Marek Hłasko, and Ireneusz Iredyński. I learned many interesting things about this period and these people, where they spent their time, what they ate, whom they socialized with, what kinds of cars they drove, what tea they bought, whether they drank coffee, how late they came home and with whom. From wiretap records, I learned about their fears and desires.

But I still couldn't get my hands on any information about Foucault himself.

Finally I typed into the search engine of one of the computers in the Institute's reading room the most obvious word in the context of Michel Foucault's time in Warsaw.

I got one hit.

I filled out a request form.

After a two-week wait, the clerk handling my case called and said:

"Mr. Ryziński, you found the right catalogue number."

The world of melancholy is damp, heavy, and cold,
while the world of mania is dry and ardent
made of both violence and fragility.

History of Madness

THE BOYS

Meeting

Waldek put on his best pants, brushed his hair, rubbed some of his father's aftershave on his cheeks, and left the house. It took him and the boys nearly an hour to drive from Saska Kępa, on Warsaw's right bank, to Okęcie Airport. It was evening—warm, because it was summer.

Foucault was waiting in the arrivals hall. Waldek smiled and held out his hand.

Waldek wanted very much to go to France. And what an opportunity: a man who came from there!

Waldek was nineteen and looked like a kid. He was just discovering the city and himself. But it was happening so fast—like an avalanche, as he puts it.

He hung out in the cafés. He had a boyfriend—Stefan—and a few close companions.

That summer evening, Waldek, Stefan, Jurek, and Mirek went to Okęcie. Later, they were joined by Henryk, whom they called "the Countess." They went from the airport back to the city center, straight to Rutkowski Street (now known as Chmielna). They threw a party. Wine, vodka, and some snacks to go with it.

This was the setup. Foucault played the host. Waldek was with Stefan. Mirek was in love with Stefan. And Jurek was single, always in high spirits, and the real soul of the group. Henryk, for his part, acted mainly as an interpreter. All he cared about was looking at and spending time with young men, that was enough to keep him happy.

Waldek and Michel gazed at each other and exchanged a few words.

Nothing happened.

Waldek's lover, Stefan, was the obstacle. So was the lack of a common language and Waldek's modesty.

Some time had to pass before finally—one balmy night—Waldek stayed over at Foucault's.

That was how it went.

Like an avalanche.

Inquisitive

In the year Foucault came to Poland, Henryk Tyrakowski, an employee of the secret police, was studying to become a major in Legionowo, outside Warsaw. He had a C in philosophy and a B in sociology. He also had a wife and three sons. His boys were sickly and his wife belligerent. Their marital conflict was suppressed "in accordance with the Party line."

Harmony was demanded and so harmony there was.

During the war, Henryk was deported along with his brother and his mother to a forced labor camp in Kolberg (today's Kołobrzeg). He worked at a bakery on a manor estate, then on the railroad. According to other Poles engaged at the Otto Werke company, it was "torture due to the brutal treatment." In a report from Tyrakowski's activities during the war—confirmed by those who'd survived—it was stated that seventeen-year-old Henryk "was very well disposed toward the Poles, but he hated the Germans, for which he was repeatedly beaten."

His patriotic convictions and friendly attitude served him in good stead for the future.

Henryk filed his first denunciation against his own brother. Describing the case, he emphasized that "any crime my aforementioned brother might potentially commit would not be motivated by hostility to the current political conditions in Poland because he is not an enemy, yet he might be taken advantage of and commit a crime due to his vices and addiction to vodka." This addiction led the brother to sell clothes and objects stolen from his family home. His behavior wore down his mother and she fell ill. This is why Henryk considered it his duty to file the denunciation. Yet his report didn't make the best impression on his superiors. They considered it to be motivated by "fear and a desire to shield himself" from the potential consequences of his brother's actions.

Still, Henryk had been noticed.

He was eager to join the secret police. In 1946 he wrote a brief note: "Please accept me as an employee of the Ministry of Public Security." And he attached an autobiographical sketch: "I come from a working-class family. My father worked in the

Żyrardów Factories as a weaver. As a young child I was given up to a children's home; I didn't enjoy a high standard of living because, as we know, conditions for workers in Poland before September '39 were appalling. The turmoil unleashed by the Teutonic invader brought an end to my studies. Then came the awful days of slavery, life under fear and terror, forced marches for a handful of kasha—all to survive. In 1940, seized by Nazi secret agents, I was deported to Germany for labor, where I remained until 1945 with my eyes cast eastward, awaiting my much anticipated liberation. In April 1945, I returned to my beloved homeland, beloved all the more for being socialist and democratic."

He considered service in the secret police his "sacred civic duty" and, without hesitation, signed a statement of commitment. He declared his loyalty to Free, Democratic, and Independent Poland and committed to the struggle against hostile elements. He wished to work with dedication and diligence, not letting slip any official secrets. He would never betray any information, whisper a word, give anything away.

Well, except in his reports, which were not betrayal, but a source of pride.

In Henryk's home, a sense of obligation toward the socialist homeland prevailed. His wife was committed to the system, their children were raised loyal to the party, without religion, and with a sense of pride and duty toward the Polish people's government.

In 1952, out of a sense of duty although without particular conviction, Henryk changed his last name and became Terakowski. He changed it to match a misspelling on his birth certificate—real life had to line up with the paperwork. In this period he also changed his handwriting. Previously, his documents had been written in tiny, elegant letters with fanciful embellishments, loops, flourishes, and dots like little circles. His reports written for the secret police lost all their embellishments and the letters became large and tilted, energetic, as if carved with a knife.

At first his assessors didn't view his work positively, and his grades were mixed at best. For discipline: C+, though he got As for political interest and quality of Polish. He had difficulty recruiting collaborators. Terakowski's network of contacts was considered weak. At the same time, he was engaged, politically conscious, and—according to some—even nationalistic. He always had a loyal attitude toward the people's democratic government. Furthermore, he was: "morally suitable, intellectual, intelligent, eager to learn. Respectful of individual rank, ideological and polite, truthful, free of addictions. Sophisticated company."

He just had no luck finding informants.

His colleagues were recruiting well-known names and influential people, while all Terakowski could get were poor little wretches.

But finally, luck smiled upon him.

He started throwing himself into his assignments and made sure to continue his education, which opened a career path for him. On July 12, 1959, he graduated from the Ministry of Internal Affairs secret police school with high marks overall. His evaluations grew more positive. He was waiting for an assignment that could show off his skills. Partly by chance and partly sensing an opportunity, he started infiltrating Warsaw's gay community.

He felt no revulsion.

He maintained his distance, of course, but he had no problem talking to young men from the city.

He had his methods.

In April 1962, he took on an operation codenamed "Patek." And at the same time, he made operational contact with Waldek, who was given the codename "Drill."

At the time Henryk was thirty-nine. Waldek was twenty-two.

And he was the first to tell Terakowski about Michel Foucault.

Saska Kępa

A narrow side street leads to Waldek's old apartment in Saska Kępa. Cars are parked on both sides. There are a few houses and apartment buildings here, built of the white stone used in wealthy neighborhoods. On the front of his building are windows and small balconies, while the entrance doors are on the side facing the courtyard, which is broad and open on all sides.

Tall poplars, locusts, Douglas firs, and arborvitaes grow here. Evergreen shrubs stand near two carpet hangers. Beneath one of the small trees in the center of the courtyard stands a small bench, cobbled together from something that wasn't a bench before (Bookshelves? Jam cupboards? No—two stools joined by a wooden plank). In good weather, this is where elderly women and men, Waldek's old friends, sit and feed the pigeons, reminiscing about the old days, how *it was better before, believe you me.*

And here and there—by the house, under the windows, behind a small fence, surrounded by creeping dwarf pines and coniferous perennials—are hydrangeas, colorful in summer, brown and dead in winter.

Waldek moved here in 1959. There was no courtyard or neighboring properties yet, but construction vehicles were already carving out the road and the sidewalk had been laid. The apartment was comfortable, large, and bright. Two rooms, a separate kitchen, bathroom, and small hallway. Almost 60 square meters! Waldek had his own bedroom with windows overlooking the street. He would spend time sitting in his room studying and sneaking kisses from his boyfriend. His mother bustled around in the kitchen and his father earned money for the household. Saska Kępa blossomed beautifully in spring.

Waldek lived there for over thirty years. When he was selling the apartment, he carefully cleared everything out, moving his parents' possessions down to the basement: boxes of photos, homemade fruit juice and plum jelly, a large tin of tea. Trash and memories.

A Communist by Conviction

After the war, Waldek's father came home a changed man. They could tell right away which direction he was heading. He believed that if everything was shared, each person would care for it equally.

"I've hated communism since I was a boy and to this day I believe in both the law and in justice," stresses Waldek. "But my father was a real communist, a patriot. And he was very sharp, he didn't work a day of his life, he just smuggled meat back and forth from Karczew."

In Waldek's telling, his father generally respected him. But when he finally did find out, he was shocked, disbelieving, threatening his son with consequences—probably fearing what people would say, fearing his boy facing an uphill battle. But in the end it all calmed down.

"My father said to me: Walduś, it's hard for me to wrap my head around you, because I know there were guys who made it with Germans, had some kind of sexual relations with them, but that's because they wanted to survive. But you've got everything, a good life, freedom, a family—and you get up to stuff like that?"

As a straight man, he just didn't get it.

All Skin and Bones

Waldek's mother did what mothers do—she loved her son more than anything.

A photo: Waldek in shorts and light-colored knee socks, clinging to a woman sitting on a stool. Further along, his brother and the ruins of Warsaw.

"We were so hungry," says Waldek, "that I used to find bones on the street and stick them in my mouth. Then they'd have to coat the inside of my throat with disinfectant."

Her whole life, Waldek's mother feared nothing except him getting hurt. It wasn't only out of love that she accepted her son's homosexuality, but also because of the danger inherent in it. You'd hear so-and-so had disappeared, so-and-so had gotten mugged, so-and-so got beat up; meaning in spite of everything, Mama Julia was glad Waldek had his Stefan.

"My mom confessed it was a tragedy for her. But she accepted it because she loved me and figured it was better with me having my one guy rather than bringing people home all the time, which would have meant danger and death hanging in the air. And shame as well."

Birthday

The poppy seed cake has been sitting out since the weekend, but it's still good.

Waldek asks if I'd like my coffee small or large. He takes two mugs out of the cabinet over the sink. Using the spoon from the sugar bowl, he drops in some instant coffee and adds a small measure of powdered cappuccino, then Cremona and a little single-serving capsule of cream. He pours boiling water over it all and hands it to me. It's early evening, Waldek shouldn't be drinking coffee now, but it helps with his digestion.

"The final slice of cake. It's better with cognac drizzled over it, but we haven't got any. It's all right this way too. My husband made it himself. He's a professional pastry chef."

His husband's most important quality is that he's never betrayed Waldek. In August they'll have been together thirty years. He looks after Waldek like no one else does. Recently he planted some sprouts, which sit on top of the fridge in a few containers: radishes, cress, lentils, and fenugreek.

Waldek wolfs down the poppy seed cake. He sips a teaspoonful of coffee. He adds sugar, because it's bitter.

He is seventy-six years old.

Foucault would be ninety.

Fifty-seven years have passed since their romance.

I jot down the numbers in my notebook: I count, subtract, and add; I play with time.

"In retrospect, that Foucault probably wasn't my type. I don't get involved with older men. I'm still the same way: I'm into the young ones, the older ones I don't care for."

Waldek is dressed warmly, despite being at home: a button-down shirt, a sweater, a vest with pockets for little treasures. Slippers on his feet. On my way in, I asked if I should take off my shoes—yes, do.

He calls his apartments an investment, because the banks are crooks. But as Lulla, one of Waldek's girlfriends, sensibly remarks:

"Oh please, what's Miss Walda going to do, take it to the grave? She should go to the spas in Ciechocinek, slather herself in clay, or mud from the Dead Sea, then she'll live another couple years, but all her 'investments' will bring her is nerves and nerves, and inside: emptiness."

The only thing Waldek fears in life is being alone.

Because sometimes it happens, of course, that someone comes along, hangs around a good while, then up and leaves you and you're on your own again. Everyone prioritizes their own life over Waldek's. Even his husband, who has to go out to the countryside, tend the crops, and bring back the tomatoes and potatoes because they won't pick themselves.

In January, Waldek celebrated his birthday. The party lasted three days, because you know how it is, oh look, your cousin came, and you've got some friends here, and your best friends there: there's no way you could get them all together at once.

Waldek rents out one of his apartments, but not the whole thing, just a room for a couple złotys, on the condition that whenever he wants he can come, hang out, chat. Recently he rented the room to a fine young man who'd had a falling-out with his girlfriend. But the couple made up. No skin off Waldek's nose since the young man had put down a deposit, it just didn't work out. That wasn't the first time anyway. Before that there'd been another straight boy: seductive, athletic. He'd bring girls home, but he was even sweet to Waldek. The first time it was all, "Stop, Waldek, what are you doing, quit fooling around," but in the end, they slept together.

"Now, my suspicion is he's got personality issues. Whenever he's in Warsaw, it's always my place he wants to sleep at, even though his mom and grandma live right nearby. They pressure him and that's why he feels this sort of hatred for women. Normally he's collected, smart, well put together, he's never tried to milk me too much. He's attracted to women, because you can tell that's what he was taught, but it's purely physical, to use them and lose them. The way it goes sometimes is, there's the sex, the physical part, but the emotional end of it is practically hatred. Because he's got psychological baggage on top of it all. From his mother and his grandma."

This straight tenant sent Waldek birthday greetings from London, saying he'd taught him more than anybody else in his life about happiness and how to live at peace with yourself.

Fifty years earlier, Waldek spent his birthday on a ship, the freighter *Romer*, sailing to the United States. It was January, cold, and the squalls were so strong people were puking their guts out over the side. There weren't many passengers; he got a two-person cabin and better conditions overall than those on the famous ocean liner M.S. *Batory.* The food on board was bad and everything stank of fish, but everyone looked past that and was really happy. Besides, what fun—sailing, an adventure!

"Three weeks at sea. More than enough time to think over us fleeing our beloved homeland and sailing to another world, which we imagined would be better. But since we didn't really know what we'd find there, it was all apprehension and the great unknown."

The only thing soothing Waldek's uncertainty and anxiety was the knowledge his beloved Stefan waited on that distant shore.

A Scandalmonger by Nature

What you needed above all to get into America was an invitation.

Stefan went first, invited by someone he used to know from Warsaw. When Waldek finally got to New York, they told the acquaintance they were brothers, but it wasn't long before he'd worked out they were actually lovers and threw them out.

The kinds of emotions and the story they shared wouldn't remain hidden or go unsaid.

Waldek had been a model student majoring in economics at Warsaw's Main School of Planning and Statistics, polite to his professors, cheerful to his friends, and charming to girls. He could never remember their names, so called them all "darling," and they would literally glow and say to one another: *that Waldek is so sweet.*

Though unfortunately for them, they were getting the wrong end of the stick.

After class he'd return home, eat dinner, and then study, read, and go through his notes. Sometimes he'd go out at night—his favorite was the Amatorska, sometimes he'd go to the Roxana, more rarely the Alhambra—but even if he did, he'd take his textbooks with him. He'd sit at a table, hide behind his books, and fantasize about someone sliding into the seat next to him, meeting someone. He was romantic and sentimental, though also clearheaded.

In the fall of 1958, Stefan spotted him.

They were different in every way. Stefan was one of Warsaw's bad boys. Big, strong, dangerous. He played sports, met lots of men and lots of women, and was trying to find his place in life. Meanwhile Waldek was dainty, delicate, fragile. He knew his goals and priorities.

"You'd get all kinds of folks mixed together at the club," he says. "Both straights and gays, though back then we didn't say 'gays,' it was usually *cioty*—'queers.' Or you might make a certain gesture with your head, or your eyes or your hands, and that was all anyone needed to get what you meant."

In this crowd of all kinds of folks, Stefan appreciated Waldek's politeness.

And Waldek, Stefan's manliness.

There was no containing it.

In retrospect, this is how Waldek sees it: he was a young man from a good home and, like so many other boys from his background, he was sexually drawn to the slums. And that's how Stefan got so deep into his heart, with that feeling of danger and masculinity.

"We met one afternoon at the Amatorska, and that same evening we went off to Poznań. We stayed in a student hostel. There was some girl hanging around there, and since Stefan was in the mood, he started coming onto her. He was extremely attractive, a swimmer, fairly sexually mature, there was a lot to like. Anyway, in what you might call his first phase, he was straight, not one of your classic queens. But, you know, you get drawn into these things, you get used to it, stuck in it like a swamp. But we couldn't shake that girl. We got on the streetcar and she followed us. So that was the first time I said to him right out: if you want to go with her, be my guest—and I hopped off the streetcar."

Stefan ran after Waldek and the girl stayed onboard. They never heard from her again.

That night, Waldek submitted to Stefan for the first time.

That's how he remembers it, at least.

Waldek has no time for modern political correctness. He talks about things the way he's always seen them: he calls his husband a "trick," and making love, "a fuck."

Hair on the Siphon

Stefan's acquaintance, the one who invited him to the United States, had been friends in Warsaw with a lieutenant colonel in the Polish Armed Forces named Stanisław Z. It was this lieutenant colonel who led to the problems between Waldek and Stefan.

And, in a way, he also caused the problems with Foucault.

Z. was found dead in his apartment in June 1961. He lay on a rug, completely naked. The emergency doctor stated the cause of death was blunt-force trauma to the head, four blows. They found drops of blood, hair, and traces of fingerprints on a siphon bottle of soda water standing on the table.

Conclusion: the siphon bottle was the murder weapon.

The investigation report stated that the lieutenant colonel was well known in the scene as a homosexual. He changed partners often, made the most of each opportunity, and frequented men's bathhouses, public urinals, and bars—most often, the Roxana and the Antyczna.

A manhunt was launched among Warsaw's homosexuals, leading to a list of suspects being drawn up.

"I met the colonel through Stefan," says Waldek. "He was an older fellow, nice, smooth, polite. He spoke a bunch of languages and did translations for the military. It's a fact he liked his boys in mass quantities. He wasn't picky or afraid of anything, and, sadly for him, that's how he got involved with 'the Weightlifter.' Now that guy was something! This giant hulk of a man, he scared the hell out of us, but everyone still wanted to get into bed with him. I saw him once through a one-way mirror during a confrontation at a police station. That time he looked anything but gorgeous, nobody from our crowd would have given him a second look."

One memory comes to Waldek's mind.

It was Midsummer—festive, delightful, not like today. Everyone was having a fabulous time. That day, the lieutenant colonel was meant to pick up some money from the bank, a large amount.

"Queer that he was, he went bragging all over the place."

He was on his way to the bank when tragedy struck: a festival platform by the harbor on the Vistula River collapsed. A host of people drowned, ambulances were racing back and forth like crazy, and the traffic was so bad the lieutenant colonel couldn't get to the bank to collect his money. He went home empty-handed, and that was when he was murdered.

Since the deceased was a soldier of the Polish Armed Forces, the investigation was meticulous. The investigators tracked down Stefan, and through him, Waldek.

And then it began.

So much torment and terror that even today it brings Waldek to tears. The police knew about Stefan's lifestyle, and given that there was a lot of money and a lieutenant colonel involved, Stefan was preemptively arrested.

He spent two weeks in custody at police headquarters. When he was released, he went straight to Waldek's in Saska Kępa. He didn't want to say anything, because he'd signed a collaboration agreement while in jail. They'd tortured him, made him stand naked for hours and hours on rocks in cold water.

"I'd imagine," ponders Waldek, "they don't use methods like that anymore—not on murderers or even on gays."

Waldek didn't expect them to come for him too. He had no direct connection, a spotless reputation, and a meek personality—what reason could they have? But they'd found men's underwear at the crime scene—the cheap, outdoor-market variety. It was evidence—all they had to do was find the owner.

The investigators scoured gay Warsaw with that underwear like the prince with Cinderella's missing slipper. Finally, they came to Saska Kępa and asked Waldek's mother: is this your son's underwear? His mother replied incredulously: bloomers like those? But they hauled him to the station: *awright you so-and-so, you were this suspect Stefan's lover, so if you want to help him out, you better sing for us—everything you know.*

Waldek *wanted* to sing, but he didn't know what about. They made him take his pants off so a dog could sniff them. Then they had him stand in a little yard next to other criminals and the dog went to him, which meant it had picked up his scent. The next day, they took Waldek to a site on the riverbank where the dog again appeared to detect his scent.

And now the policemen were positive Waldek had been up to something, though he himself didn't know what.

As Waldek sees it: here you have an educated, polite, well-mannered person, one with what you might call a proper upbringing, and you've got him lying on a jailhouse floor like some murderer or worse.

They interrogated him for many hours: you whore, you faggot, spit it out, what do you know, how'd you do it?

Waldek was on the verge of psychological collapse, so he readied a razor. He hid it in his sock and sobbed: *God, if you exist . . .*

Today he thinks the police, firstly, had nothing on him and, secondly, must have had hidden cameras and microphones in his cell. Because how else could he explain why, after praying out loud, the policemen let him go? Waldek's main memory of those forty-eight hours of his life is that they were gruesome.

Worst of all: when the investigators walked past him, they'd spit on him like he was a whore.

Recruitment

It was while the lieutenant colonel's case was going on that Waldek first gathered information for the police. He'd go to the Antyczna, the Roxana, the Lajkonik, and pepper everyone with questions—though he never had any idea what to ask about.

On April 21, 1962, secret police agent Henryk Terakowski knocked on the door of Waldek's apartment in Saska Kępa. He had an operation carefully planned out. Based on prior intelligence, he already knew that Waldek Ś. had Polish citizenship and ethnicity, an engineering degree, and a working-class social background. His documents listed his "current social position" as: *intelligentsia*. Under "Party membership": *non-Party*. In addition: a bachelor, no criminal record, no previous work with other intelligence agencies. Terakowski had a photograph of Waldek and a description: boyish looks, naïve eyes, side-parted auburn hair, an oval face, short stature. There were two options for the terms of recruitment: voluntary and coerced. For Waldek, it read: voluntary.

The agent knew Waldek was homosexual and on that basis had picked him out as a potential lure in a case he was leading against a Frenchman, codenamed "Patek."

But the source he'd uncovered was even more valuable than he'd realized.

He Was Big and in Plainclothes

Waldek clearly remembers that scene in the apartment in Saska Kępa.

Terakowski was large and strong, while Waldek was slight, apprehensive, uncertain. Terakowski threatened to out Waldek to his family, told him that he wouldn't find work, that he'd die in prison, that you can always pin something on somebody. That they'd finish him off and his parents too, if they had to.

Waldek and I are sitting at the living room table. This is not the living room where his meeting with Terakowski took place. Waldek is serving communist-era tea he recently dug out from among his mementos in the basement. He explains that back then, tea wasn't just right there, at arm's reach—so you bought it in bulk, didn't drink a lot, re-steeped the same tea leaves over and over, and poured the leftovers together into one container to make a blend. And some of those blends are better than the tea you can buy everywhere today. One tea gives color, another flavor, so a blend is best. This tea is strong, doesn't leave stains on the glass, and has a smoky aftertaste. Or maybe it's dust, who knows.

Tea, Waldek continues, should be served in a glass, to leave the color visible. So we drink from glasses. Waldek also shows me a tea service from the old government-run folk art company. Each cup is unique, hand-painted, more or less the same pattern, but there are differences in the details. Waldek has a full set that he keeps in a display case and brings out for special occasions, while day-to-day he drinks out of an ordinary mug. For occasions in between, there are the glasses.

Waldek sketches out the apartment in Saska Kępa with a trembling hand. The walls, windows, and arrows resemble a child's tracings. First he draws an overall map, marking the streets, his room, the kitchen, and the entrance. He comments on everything out loud, fusses, describes, and persuades him-self it was exactly like this, no different.

Memory is only imagination.

Finally, he marks a table against the wall in the living room, and draws large circles—chairs.

"We sat here. Him with his back to the room, me by the wall. He was big, legs spread wide, like he was sitting on a horse. He was smoking a cigarette. I kept quiet."

Terakowski had come in plainclothes. He always came in plainclothes. This first time, the air was heavy with terror. Waldek's mother was home—she hid in the kitchen. It all lasted no longer than an hour.

In his declaration, Waldek wrote: "I the undersigned Wal-demar Ś. undertake to perform tasks for the agencies of the Security Service within the scope of establishing information to confirm (to the best of my ability) that the individual indi-cated to me is a homosexual. I undertake to present detailed and truthful accounts of sexual acts that have occurred with the individual indicated. I resolve to keep the above aggree-ment in strict confidence from any and all others. I have been warned of the punitive consequences in the event of violating confidentiality. I undertake to perform the abovementioned tasks and other tasks of this nature as required, in the aware-ness that the Security Agency will assist me."

The Report on Foucault

Before Waldek was introduced in detail to the "Patek" case for which he had been recruited, Terakowski requested he give precise and comprehensive information on persons known to him, particularly homosexuals. He told Waldek to make special note of foreigners.

A few days later, Waldek gave Terakowski a memorandum he had prepared. He wanted to have something to show, he wanted them to leave him alone and in peace, so he considered this first batch of information particularly important. He therefore cast his memory back to 1959 and described the only foreigner he knew at that time: Michel Foucault.

"Probably in the summer of 1959 I learned my friend had gotten to know a Frenchman by the name of Foucault. Because I knew a little French it was decided I should meet him. This then occurred. At a time when Foucault was to return by plane from Paris, Stefan O., Jurek R., and I went to the airport to welcome the foreigner (I stress they both already knew Foucault). Upon greeting him, we all went to Foucault's residence on Rutkowski Street. At the apartment I also found Henryk R., whom I had known for some time and with whom I was very close despite our difference in age. I returned to Foucault's apartment several days in a row. Each day, I found the company I mentioned above, though with small changes because, as I realized, this foreigner was a homosexual who enjoyed changing his 'bed boys' fairly frequently. Despite our acquaintance, nothing intimate transpired between me and Foucault in the course of those days because of Stefan, who was my close friend and in front of whom it was unsuitable to do anything. We were only intimate once Stefan had left Warsaw with Mirek from Mazowsze, since they had met in that apartment and, I felt, were mutually attracted. I then spent the night at Foucault's and relations took place between us, naturally at my companion's initiative. I only returned to the apartment another few times, to the point that I was not even aware of when Foucault had left Poland. I of course learned of his departure, but only later from friends."

In a secret police memorandum prepared the day after his meeting with Waldek, Terakowski wrote: "The Foucault referred to in this report is a former French lecturer at UW. Currently 'Drill' maintains no contact with him. However, he knows from acquaintances that Foucault currently lives in Paris with a friend/lover of his."

That "friend/lover" was Daniel Defert, Foucault's partner. Waldek had learned this from Jurek, who used to look after Foucault's apartment and knew him best back then.

Jurek

There's not much that can be said about Jurek.

Perhaps only that he was born, he lived, and he died—prematurely. Someone looking back might say he had two great successes in life: the Countess and Foucault.

Jurek wrote an autobiographical statement when he was applying for a job with the performance ensemble of the Ministry of Internal Affairs. He declared that in 1958 he'd passed the entrance exam to the State Theater College in Warsaw, then dropped out a year later and gone to Gdańsk, where he'd sometimes performed at the Rapsodyczny Theater. He was young, good-looking, and talkative. The world was his for the taking, yet he quickly realized that neither a diploma nor even a stage could guarantee him popularity—only the proper contacts could.

After returning to Warsaw, Jurek performed at various theaters as supporting roles, replacements, and understudies. In the evenings, he did popular cabaret shows at the Adria, the Kameralna, and the Astoria.

But he never broke into the top tier of the stage world.

No theater archive has any mention of him, except one saying he was once an understudy for an actor in the chorus.

An opinion from the manager of one of the theaters where Jurek had worked: "He made himself known as an employee with mediocre acting skills."

Another theater fired him because instead of acting in the show, he'd accepted a well-paid, one-time job performing in a program in honor of Lenin's birthday.

He'd hoped that would be a mitigating circumstance.

It was not.

When they went to meet Foucault at the airport, it was Jurek who brought the keys to the Frenchman's apartment on Rutkowski Street. Whenever Michel was away, he would leave the place to Jurek, with the refrigerator full. A few times, Jurek invited guests over and threw raucous, drunken parties. One event that attained mythical status was an orgy including two (female) prostitutes who were secret police plants.

Yet Foucault trusted this boy who had no money, no job, who didn't know French—whose mind swirled with dreams of a spectacular career, of photos, lights, and champagne.

Yet no grand stage and no champagne ever featured in Jurek's life. More often, it was despair and vodka.

Legends circulated about the holes in the walls of Jurek's apartment. These were drilled through the inside of a wardrobe from the living room to the bathroom. They were peepholes. When a soldier or workman came to the apartment, Jurek would tell them to take a shower, claiming he was very clean and a stickler for cleanliness in others. The young man would go to the bathroom, undress, wash, and behave unselfconsciously. Meanwhile, Jurek would go into the wardrobe and bask in the joys of voyeurism.

"It was awfully emotional," recalls one witness. "Watching this soldier take off his uniform, pull off his suspenders, and climb into the tub naked. It's what added spice to the whole story. As for spending the night, so what? They did their thing, turned their asses to one another, and went to sleep."

Jurek was a bachelor, but at the age of twenty-eight he adopted a boy—Maciej.

To this day, how he managed to do that remains a great mystery.

The adoption was "full and complete," meaning the total severance of any links between the adopted child and his biological family, while his new guardian's status was permanent. Jurek was therefore a father by law—though in real life, not so much.

Jurek's mother looked after the child. The mother, Jurek, and Maciej have all passed away. No one can explain the true story of the adoption. Jurek's granddaughter never met her grandfather. Today, she recalls her family saying "he wasn't an interesting person."

"My father didn't actually talk about his family, and my mom didn't ask," says Zuzanna. "It seems like he was aware he was adopted and didn't spend time worrying about it. But it's unclear to us why the family decided to adopt a child and how it was possible. Unless by some accident this Jurek was his biological father? Then why would they put off the adoption for three years? My father believed he was about that age when he was adopted, because he had flashes of memories from the orphanage."

Zuzanna knows her grandfather was gay, though that wasn't spoken about at home either. She never thought to dig into the past, but in the end, she wonders if maybe it's worth doing.

Today, only one person lays flowers at Jurek's grave in Bródno Cemetery: an old acquaintance from the Alhambra club, Andrzej. He doesn't know how all this was possible either.

How did solitary Jurek come to adopt Maciej?

Why was he the one with the keys to Michel Foucault's apartment?

Was this the Jurek who caused Foucault to leave?

Andrzej, like everyone else, only remembers vodka on the table first thing in the morning, all-night drinking bouts, and peepholes in the wardrobe through which Jurek used to watch naked soldiers.

The Countess

The closest friend Jurek made was Henryk, nicknamed "the Countess."

The Countess—born in January 1912—was not aristocratic in the slightest. He knew many people, visited many people's homes, and for one reason or other everyone thought the

Countess's blood really was blue. Maybe it was because of his manners, which were excellent. He also spoke flawless French. He wore a morning coat with striped pants and minced around like a dandy. He was the picture of a nobleman.

There are two types of people who knew him: those who didn't know he had no real title and those who didn't know how he earned his living.

The Countess's name and address appear in Michel Foucault's private notebook from this period. Nothing connected them beyond friendly and free-flowing conversation. Foucault's everyday life in Warsaw was divided into his daytime, professional routine and his evening, recreational one. At work in the Center of French Culture, he could only talk about philosophy and literature. Meanwhile, he was still young and single, and also interested in young men and madness.

He was on the lookout for after-dark opportunities, but then language was an obstacle. He didn't know how to make himself understood to the young men of the city. So maybe, out of all of Michel's Polish acquaintances, it was Countess Henryk—a Francophile of the old school, a young spirit curious about the world—who introduced him to the street life of Warsaw?

In at least one case, this was certainly so.

Henryk was very insistent that his charge, Jurek, should move in good circles. He knew the boy was not graced with talent, but he was handsome and sociable. The authors Jarosław Iwaszkiewicz and Jerzy Andrzejewski, the composer Zygmunt Mycielski, the poet Paweł Hertz—they each had a boy of their own. So Henryk wanted a boy of his own, too. He introduced his Jurek to Michel Foucault and turned a blind eye to their romance, then ultimately was only ever with them when functioning as an interpreter.

When Michel and Jurek were alone, they could understand each other without words.

"He was a real somebody," says an old friend of Henryk's. "People used to give him a little bow when he walked into a café or the Messalka bathhouse on Krakowskie Przedmieście. Which he did often. Because there, the Countess was the queen of the joint. She was well-known, distinguished, and openhanded, so young boys gathered around her, boys who were on scholarships or not on scholarships, in any case ones who weren't earning much or got paltry allowances. The Countess would always take them for dinner, for coffee—in a word, she would help out. While her relationship with Foucault was close, it definitely wasn't physical."

Little information about Henryk R. can be found at the Institute of National Remembrance. His passport files only indicate numerous journeys—with his wife and children. Under "profession" it reads: *man of letters*, which perhaps encompassed most broadly the Countess's innumerable talents.

According to information from Division 8 of Department 2 of the Ministry of Internal Affairs, from 1958 to 1971 Henryk maintained "extensive contacts" with employees of the French Embassy. He went to receptions and cocktail parties and met privately with representatives of Francophile organizations, doubtless including Michel Foucault.

Many people say Henryk was a wonderful character: loving and admirable, friendly and helpful in every situation. The only competition he had was Karol Hanusz—the cabaret artist known as the King of the Roxana.

Mirek from Mazowsze

The secret police notes on Mirek cover the whole of the 1960s. That was when Mirek was at the height of his career in the Mazowsze State Folk Song and Dance Ensemble. He traveled abroad, fell in love with Stefan, and through him met Michel Foucault.

In one photograph Mirek has a long, oval face, very pale, a long nose, eyes with straight brows, fairly thin lips, large ears, a high forehead, with high, upswept blond hair.

A romantic look.

Agent "Zygmunt" reported that Mirek was a "very hard-working, conscientious, and dutiful" young man, which he considered surprising given the dancer's young age. Unfortunately, despite his discipline and hard work, in the agent's mind he wasn't suited as a soloist. Perhaps not even for want of talent, but rather due to "the strong competition and his delicacy of character." In addition, the agent noted, "the boy's life lacks order and he is politically immature." On international trips he was "well-behaved and cause[d] no trouble."

Mirek was so modest and quiet that his male colleagues from the ensemble made fun of him, so by day he preferred the company of women.

"He really did stick with the girls," says Maria Jopek, a soloist in Mazowsze who was friends with Mirosław. "But you could tell there was no more to it than that. We knew Mirek was looking for a different kind of relationship."

That's why his marriage to the daughter of one of socialist Warsaw's few successful capitalists came as such a surprise. It shocked his friends from the Roxana, but no one said a word.

Such marriages were common in those days.

Mirek's close friend from Mazowsze, Marek Keller—Jerzy Andrzejewski's lover and today a philanthropist and donor to institutions including the Fryderyk Chopin Museum in Warsaw—adds that Mirosław was a favorite of Mira Zimińska-Sygietyńska, who took the reins of the ensemble in 1957 and became its icon. As manager, she frequently defended him from the aspersions of his colleagues and the schemes of the secret police.

"Mrs. Zimińska was an institution," says Keller. "Whenever the latest denunciation arrived, she'd take the person in question to one side and tear up the paper in front of them, without reading it. And she loved gay men. Nothing surprised her, because in that profession it went without saying."

Not everyone thought that way. One comment in Mirek's file is a handwritten note from an agent, asking (we don't know whom): "Can't we chase these types out of Mazowsze?"

Another agent, "Krzysiek," describing the ensemble's American tour, noted of Mirek: "One of the most active homosexuals. He has had a large number of contact with men in nearly every city. As he left one city, he would obtain similar types of contacts to men in the next. He constantly went around with them at night. He received gifts and money from them. He made friends with a homosexual through an American producer. [. . .] Politically, he gives an impression of devotion to People's Poland. In discussing the matter of 'how things are in Poland,' he always defends his country. He has had a rather ironic relationship with the Americans. These contacts of [Mirek's] prompted fear that he might stay in the United States or someplace similar, where he could arrange for the others to work. That was our impression, of fear."

Nothing connected him to Foucault apart from Stefan. He loved Stefan so much that the fact he was with Waldek made the young dancer want to throw himself under a train. Foucault hardly crossed the boys' minds at that time, because they were caught in their love triangle.

Many years later, Waldek ran into Mirek on the street. He remembers Mirek cut a handsome figure, of course, being a dancer. He was tall, even potentially attractive.

"But he was effeminate, you could work out he was a fairy." And to Waldek, masculinity mattered above all else.

The Boys from the Report

They all met with Foucault:

The Countess, because he knew the language,

Jurek, because he knew the Countess,

Waldek, because he wanted to go to France,

Stefan, because he liked a good time,

And Mirek, because he followed Stefan everywhere.

Everyone in Warsaw knew each other anyway. It was a close-knit community. So they also knew Michel Foucault. People would say: that Frenchman, you know. And everyone did know.

But these were the boys from the city who were closest to him.

Henryk, Jurek, and Mirek have since passed away.

Waldek and Stefan continue to feel a great passion for one another. But their love has transformed into its exact opposite.

The Job

Maybe it was Waldek's love of masculinity that complicated things, made them spin out of control.

Waldek and secret police agent Henryk Terakowski met once again at Pod Arkadami café on a May afternoon in 1962. Waldek arrived early, which Terakowski interpreted as a sign of eagerness to collaborate—all the more so because Waldek kept impatiently asking when he'd be able to get the job started.

"You've got to keep waiting. Be patient."

"But I haven't got time, I've got plans. I want to get the job over with as quickly as possible, so I can go to France on vacation."

"To France, you say?"

"That's right. And I expect help arranging a passport. One good turn deserves another."

"We'll see. Once you've done the job, we won't raise any objections."

That alone was plenty. Waldek wanted to be sure and asked Terakowski to show him his badge; the agent interpreted this as a sign of mistrust and duplicity on the young man's part. He gave Waldek a stern reprimand, then set the date for their next meeting.

Waldek didn't show.

Then he explained he'd had class at the university and

couldn't. It was a dangerous game. Terakowski made it extremely clear Waldek was not to miss a meeting again. He also showed the young man an official summons to the station, in case he had any more doubts. Waldek remembered what a summons like that meant; it resolved any doubts he had.

The job would be this:

"On the 11ᵗʰ of this month, 'Drill' will begin the assignment. It will be conducted on the grounds of the orchestra hall. He has been ordered to dress appropriately. 'Drill' was eager to accept the assignment. He asked for a few złotys to buy a suitable tie for his suit, since he did not possess one. He was given 100 zł. 'Drill' was cautioned—in the form of advice and warnings—that total loyalty was essential. 'Drill' took this warning very seriously. He declared that by signing the commitment he had documented his loyalty and would maintain it, and he is also aware that in the event of conflict between us, he will lose."

Waldek was given a ticket to the Philharmonic. The program was exceptional: Paul Kletzki was conducting, accompanied by Andor Földes on piano; the tenor was Zdzisław Nikodem and the female solos were sung by Krystyna Szostek-Radkowa. Waldek committed to memory the photos the agent had shown him. He had been informed where his target would be sitting.

He went to the concert.

He greatly enjoyed the music.

He didn't spot his target.

The day after the operation at the Philharmonic, Waldek met with Terakowski. He swore he hadn't been able to perform the job because hadn't seen Foucault anywhere.

At that moment the agent saw he'd overestimated Waldek after all.

The target of the operation at the Philharmonic hadn't been Michel Foucault, but one of Foucault's old colleagues from the embassy, René P.

Terakowski never asked to meet Waldek again.

Nothing More

"I was smart enough to pretend to be stupid and crazy," says Waldek. "At intermission I walked around looking all over the place, but did it in a way that everyone backed away like I was out of my mind. I was disgusted with the secret police for what they'd done to me and Stefan. I was naïve, but they'd abused us so horribly and then on top of it all wanted me to do them favors."

Henryk Terakowski emphasized in his last report from November 1962 that Waldek was a "sexual deviant—a homosexual. We had planned to present him the target code-named 'Patek,' who is also a homosexual. He accepted the assignment without complaint. Though an unideological person, he is legally supportive of the present political situation. Hungry for thrills and adventure. Currently not being utilized."

His file was ultimately closed in 1970.

"To me it's an interesting chapter of my life story," concludes Waldek and takes a bite of poppy seed cake.

"And nothing more?"

"Nothing."

A Vow

Waldek's first passport photo: a young man, a boy. A kid. Dark hair, his long bangs brushed back, forehead bare. And then his eyebrows—thick, dark, severe. But that's misleading, because on the whole Waldek seems like a very serene, gentle young man. He was eighteen and probably got his photos taken for his passport and national ID at the same time. In that ID photo and the one after it, only a year older, he poses in right profile. He has a very small, elegant nose and a delicate, coy mouth.

He wears a white button-down shirt, a tightly knotted dark tie and a V-neck sweater. Waldek holds still and gazes at one spot. He freezes and waits for the flash. Click. Passport photo ready.

America was his one chance to land on his feet. A trip to the U.S. cost almost a year's salary, but people finagled various ways of going, because the investment could pay for itself many times over. Waldek brought a diamond with him that he later sold, to keep him from hitting rock bottom. During his interview at the consulate he showed them a contract with his employer and his master's thesis with a special commendation, titled: *Development of the Production and Consumption of Food Concentrates in Poland, 1956–1960*.

"I predicted the consumption of concentrates based on the latest economic method: extrapolation. My essay got them to amend a couple years to match my calculations. It was prospective, with a massive bibliography. That was what got me my visa. I told the consul I'd a signed contract and for Westerners a contract is hugely significant. That's how I went. And I was supposed to come back, to go for just three months. But I stayed. I figured the best option was to get married, to stay legally. And that's what I did. I arranged a permanent stay from the American end, and I applied for a passport from the Polish authorities on the basis of my marriage."

Waldek's wife, Józefa, was thirty-two years older—a seamstress by trade, childless.

"Did we get along? She was just on paper, not real. Which is the kind of relationship it was, just based on the marriage."

On July 9, 1968 Waldek returned his passport and went back to Poland. He promised a friend in the U.S. that he'd come again for the bicentennial of American independence. But it wasn't to be. They didn't let him out again.

To France

After coming back from the U.S., Waldek and Stefan's relationship soured. They no longer needed one another and their love went cold.

Waldek brought three Volkswagens back with him. One for himself, a second for his father, a third to sell. Officially he couldn't bring American dollars into the country, so the cars were a way around the law. He sold one car for 240,000 złotys and bought an apartment next to his parents.

In those days they called him "Miss America."

"I was surrounded by girlfriends. Let's say a normal person earned a thousand złotys a month, but I could get a hundred or a hundred and twenty złotys for a single dollar, so I could afford anything, which meant so many boys wanting to get friendly that I could have my pick of the litter."

In 1972, Waldemar wanted to take a month to travel around Europe, through West Germany, the Netherlands, and Switzerland to France. Unfortunately, the passport office denied his request. The justification: "In 1964 the applicant was temporarily in the U.S.A.—he declared a three-month stay, but remained for three-and-a-half years—he entered into a marriage with a much older person, from whom he is currently separated."

Waldek had expected this, so he already had an appeal prepared. In it he asked them to reexamine his case carefully and reminded them he had repeatedly traveled abroad, "never in any way violating my professional obligations nor harming the reputation of my homeland, People's Poland." He added that he had returned from the U.S. voluntarily, "wishing to contribute and, through my labor, uphold the pillars of my beloved Socialist homeland." This declaration convinced the passport office to grant permission and Waldek, thirteen years after meeting Foucault, could finally go to France.

He got behind the wheel of his light-blue American Volkswagen 1600 TL, with his friend Janusz beside him. Destination: Paris. Living there was a Warsaw friend of his from days of yore: Rudolf.

Rudolf, meanwhile, had two close friends in the French capital: Roland Barthes and Michel Foucault.

Janusz

Janusz's apartment resembles a little souvenir shop.

Every centimeter of the compact interior overflows with knickknacks, souvenirs, and keepsakes from numerous trips. Plastic dolls, framed postcards, religious images. Artificial ivy winds between the displays. Paintings in gilt and plastic frames show flowers and vases. In the corner, a sofa with embroidered cushions on it. Through the door, a stereo tower. Here and there, photographs of beautiful men. Some originals, others Hollywood pictures. In a display case, figurines: Chinese, faïence, and ones made of handcrafted glass. Colorful birds, sky-blue with yellow beaks and rumps, ducklings in blue aprons, cowboys and little dogs smoking pipes. Pinned to the rainbow curtains in the window are linen butterflies, painted in dazzling, intense colors that might really exist in the tropics. Further along are female mannequin heads with hats, styled hair, and lipstick; a picture of the Thrice Admirable Mother of God; and a gold-painted plaster Piłsudski with a white mustache. Behind glass on the highest shelf: a Polish white eagle with a round clock in its stomach, wings spread proudly, a crown on its head. In front of the eagle: a flock of yellow-and-blue chicks and an owl. In a word: everything.

A large cat—Pusia—lounges in an armchair. A glistening coffee table stands against the wall: seemingly of real wood, but actually plywood, with a lower shelf for magazines: *Gala, Viva, Lady of the House.*

It's summer, so Janusz is wearing a Caribbean shirt and brown knee-length shorts with a yellow print. On his head sits an American baseball cap, also yellow, with a large brim and

sports team logos emblazoned on it. On his feet are leather sandals and brown socks. In his hand he holds a small electric fan.

Janusz speaks in proverbs. He can turn every sentence into
a *bon mot* or draw an anecdote out of it. When asked his age,
he replies:

"Goodness gracious! Remind me, Pusia. At present, I am
a lady without age. If you were to serve me a cake with a full
complement of candles, it would come tumbling down like the
Tower of Babel."

Janusz's mother was an actress—his father, a butcher. War,
says Janusz, is good business for a butcher. His grandfather
had known that and sent four of his sons to work in a meat
processing plant, keeping the fifth at home to inherit the land.
After the war, Janusz wound up in an orphanage in Łódź,
where there was a boarding school. He completed five years of
vocational school, was assigned a job in Warsaw, and returned
to the capital.

"Since I was unmarried, childless, not tilling the soil, and
not even much of a car afficionado, I instead bought an apartment and went to see the world."

So here sits Janusz, amid his photos from around the globe,
mementos, cooling his sweaty face with an electric fan, in his
three-room apartment with a full kitchen: one room for Janusz,
a guest room, and a third, just in case, for an especially dear
friend.

It was a long time before he accepted himself. He still hasn't
come out to his family.

He used to be afraid he might have a certain "intonation,"
which he suppressed. Only after finishing his military service
did he come to know this side of himself—and like it.

Otherwise he let nothing show.

"I'll tell you as far as I remember. The year is 1957, I'm out of the army. I'm twenty-something. I've been learning, to a certain extent, the ins and outs of my new life. When I tell my girlfriends about all this nowadays, they listen to me like I'm telling the legend of the Iron Wolf of Vilnius. It wasn't like it is now, where two fellows get together, begin to share their lives, and even move in together. Goodness, there was no living together! The best you'd get was a public toilet, no one gave the slightest thought to marriage."

Janusz calls the Warsaw gay world of the fifties "the underground." He's reluctant to think back to those times, except to joke about them. Because you can joke about anything, he claims. And if not, you can always "fly off into the world."

"In commie days I saw all of Europe. If you had a hundred dollars you could get out to the West. Waldek had a car. A Volkswagen! So I'd tell him: let's go West and see what all the fuss is about."

From Paris they brought back free pamphlets for men about sports and travel, stashing them under the floormats of the car. And among their pages, between the covers, they hid gay drawings and photos.

Janusz has a few dozen albums of photographs. He turns the pages slowly.

"Once I had youth and beauty; I am told a scrap of the latter still remains. This one here was a love of mine, we still know one another. He's a girlfriend from Wrocław, a police officer who used to pay me visits. He was in active service. But I think they suspected he was one of the family since he was supposedly a policeman but, if you please, he just sat in that window at the station and let petitioners in and only had to say: *Do you have an appointment, ma'am?* No, not ma'am, pardon me, it was *do you have an appointment, comrade?*"

Janusz says Waldek was a girlfriend, and Stefan had sexy legs.

They would meet up at the Amatorska and Janusz remembers the two of them sharing stories about Foucault.

"I only heard that Stefan had a French lover, but I never met him because I didn't want to get into the middle of all that. Besides, I had no interest in yammering away in cafés. My interests were greater: art, the stage, I loved theater, cinema. That was what attracted me and what I poured my time and money into. And also, if I may say so, boys—straight boys. But sitting with queens in coffee shops was never my sort of thing. I only know that there was some Foucault or other, but I didn't hear anything more about him, because I didn't care to."

He talks about life in the People's Republic.

About meeting boys.

About love that's unstable and always leaves you unsatisfied.

"I've never known happiness," he says after a long moment. "Unhappiness, that I do know. From life passing you by so quickly. I've had my fair share of liaisons: but what does it matter if I've stayed in touch with those men, fundamentally one ends up alone. I'm too old to pair up with anybody. I've always had young partners. I have always preferred to lose the young than to find the old. I see from all my solitary girlfriends that ours is a lost generation. Your life can never be as you would wish, and it pains you. Even the younger ones, those who are about sixty today, can't live like these kids in their twenties. Because, you see, everything is different, they meet, they go to some club with a few hundred people, and while you might well find yourself in some shaky one-night-stand, it's nothing like how it used to be. You can't even compare. And so life has passed you by, you're fundamentally alone. And that's what unhappiness is."

According to Waldek, the police could do anything they wanted.

"Nothing strange about it," he recalls. "They picked up people all the time, they didn't care about them. They were so brutal that if you just went into the bushes, even really just for a call of nature, some cop would appear out of nowhere and right away start in with: what are you up to, you prick, looking for victims?! And then beatings, interrogations, detention for twenty-four or forty-eight hours. All perfectly legal."

One afternoon Waldek turned off Zieleniecka Street into the park. There was a French-style public urinal there, meaning a semi-enclosed cylinder you stood around, like at a pillory. They called them "mushrooms."

Waldek went under the mushroom to relieve himself. Two undercover police came in: and what are you doing here, sir? Waldek said he was urinating. But they didn't believe him, and were being aggressive because they knew it was a cruising spot. They took him to the station. They confiscated his Volkswagen. And it all started again.

Waldek knew what what was coming. He went into the interrogation room and said:

"I have no intention of waiting. I'm on my way home from work, I'm married, and I can only imagine I've ended up here by mistake!"

After confirming Waldek's declaration, the officers approached him differently. They showed him pictures of homosexual men and asked:

"Do you know this guy? What about this one?"

Waldek had the same answer to everything:

"No, I don't. I don't know them! That crowd doesn't interest me. I'm married!"

And it was true.

Not for Him

So Waldek isn't surprised that Foucault couldn't adjust, nor that he encountered what he did, meaning shame and a forced departure from Poland.

"It wasn't for him. Gay life in those days wasn't at the level it is now. People would meet wherever: urinals, parks, train stations. We were scared and more than one of my friends paid for their love with their lives. The ones getting killed were mostly into butch guys, and usually had a weakness for the bottle too. I know because I knew queens like that. Sometimes one of these butch guys would be into me and it'd turn out he'd robbed somebody or even killed him. You'd get victimized by a thief or a murderer, but people would still say you were a pervert so you deserved it. How could anyone stand it?"

There are of course real dangers of oversimplification here.
The world of madness was not uniform during the classical age.
And while it would not be untrue to say that the mad were treated purely
and simply as prisoners of the police,
it would not be telling the whole truth either.

History of Madness

THE DOSSIERS

The List

On May 26, 1962, Agents "Drill," "Mirek," and "Marek" delivered a report to the intelligence services on the subject of persons "practicing homosexuality." There was a list of sixty-eight men, as well as eight women with "inclinations toward lesbian love."

The report is four typed pages.

On the left, a name—on the right, a short description.

A red X has been placed beside the details of certain well-known men. (There are no Xs by the women's names.)

Additional information has been added in blue ballpoint pen: parents' names, dates of birth, address. There is also a note at the bottom of the list about gathering places for "this category of person."

First on the list—with an X and a description—is the music critic Jerzy Waldorff.

Apart from him, there are eighteen men with red Xs and handwritten notes, ten with just handwritten notes, thirty-two with no X or note, and one with neither, crossed out in red ink: the playwright Jerzy Zawieyski.

The women include four actors, a dancer, a stage director, a journalist, a designer, and a secretary who is also noted as a "kept woman."

Michel Foucault is not on this list. Yet people are listed whom Foucault doubtless knew, as well as other French friends of his: Christian J. and René P.

Dozens of such lists were drawn up around this time.

Materials on Individuals

The dossiers are titled: *Homosexual Community: Materials on Individuals 1961-1962.*

They lay, rubber-banded together and prepared, in my pigeonhole on a shelf in the Institute of National Remembrance reading room. I looked at them nervously—there they were in front of me, within reach, yet I feared they might vanish into thin air, like Foucault himself in Warsaw.

There was something unreal about them.

The archivist unhurriedly checked the call slip.

She wrote the case number in her notebook.

She asked me to sign.

Finally I took the dossiers. I sat down at a small table.

For a moment I simply gazed at them. And then I opened the first one.

Then came the ones after that.

Four files, hundreds of pages.

They are over fifty years old, brown with age. No one before me has read them. A half-century ago someone wrote a title on each one in blue ballpoint pen, described each piece of information, created a table of contents, and grouped each person according to his significance and usefulness.

Someone categorized these people.

Researched their intimate lives.

And then wrapped rubber bands around the dossiers and put them on the shelf.

Maybe that person thought they'd stay shelved forever.

Family Photos

The dossiers lie right from the start.

The documents preserved in them do not relate only to the year 1962 and do not exclusively cover homosexuals. Previous years are also recorded, as well as often completely incidental people who in some baffling way "fall into the category."

These are yellowing and graying papers of the kind filling every home, every drawer, cupboard, or desk—hidden, valuable, but forgotten, passed on to subsequent generations for reasons no one truly knows. History recorded in reports, notes, letters, photographs. Everywhere names, pseudonyms, and titles: major, colonel, captain. And abbreviations:

KP: *Kontakt poufny*—confidential contact. OZ: *Osoba*

zaufana—trusted person. TW: *Tajny współpracownik*—secret collaborator. OI: *Osoba informująca*—informant. LK: *Lokal kontaktowy*—contact venue.

Stories typed or handwritten, full of dates and places, names and connections, meetings, relationships, breakups, love, and suffering.

Reading them felt like flipping through someone's family photo album.

Four folders of the most intimate, personal, often embarrassing information about people, most of whom have no political connection whatsoever.

None of these people was remotely dangerous.

They were sometimes peripheral figures, entirely ordinary.

Or sometimes exceptional and widely known.

Folders of homosexuals, lists of names.

Including Michel Foucault's.

Hyacinth

Many people in Poland know about the operation conducted in the 1980s and afterward code-named "Hyacinth," during which a national register of homosexuals was compiled. The reports that came out of this operation are said to amount to more than ten thousand files, a mind-boggling number. All are said to be full of information about the lives and intimate relations of people who were completely unremarkable apart from their sexual orientation. Described, clarified, and grouped somewhere—the files have since disappeared.

They were either destroyed or well hidden.

For years they have captured the imagination of those who know they exist. Many wonder where they could be and what they contain.

To this day the case remains unexplained, as if the files were a myth.

But this evidence I had found was irrefutable.

I made a table based on the secret police lists: name, date of birth, parents' names and places of birth and residence, social background, training and profession, personal connections, source of information about the person, the agents' notes.

I added a column: my own notes and questions.

Once I'd exceeded three hundred names, I stopped filling out my table.

I felt like one of them.

Volume One

The first dossier is peculiar.

It contains "general reports" on incidental or well-known people. These aim to compile as much information as possible. There is no obvious logic or set order. Surely no one anticipated there being more material.

Yet its most important element is not the materials from the "thorough study" of individual persons, but rather the reports on the general phenomenon of homosexuality in the 1950s and '60s. The goal here was to define homosexuality as an illness, and then provide "case studies."

How similar to Foucault's theory: only when a certain thing is described is it brought into existence. There were no madmen until someone named them and recorded them as such.

There were no homosexuals in Poland until someone started keeping files on them.

Evidentiary Basis

The next three volumes of the "homosexual dossiers" get into more precise descriptions of particular people—incidental, private individuals who potentially knew someone prominent, made friends with someone, or would meet them for tea or sex. These people's sole misdeed was being gay.

The collection begins, "Register of Homosexuals from Warsaw, by Name." It details twenty-seven men: actors, dancers, journalists, writers, and military officers. Some of them are bachelors, a large share are married men, a few are divorcés. One of the categories in the table is "evidentiary basis," in other words: the source of information about the individual's homosexuality. Sometimes the word "self-professed" appears here. Another possibility is "operational intelligence." But most often the source is a denunciation.

For instance, Mieczysław G.'s homosexuality is known from a letter written by his mother and a testimony from witness N.

I managed to work out witness N.'s identity. After a few months I tracked him down and asked him why he'd done it. He said that's what everyone did who got caught and was interrogated by the police. So when the officers came for him, he decided there was no way out and he named the homosexuals he knew of—not only the ones he knew personally.

They included some famous figures, like the writer Jarosław Iwaszkiewicz. "I mean," he explains, "everyone knew about him anyway."

There were many gay men who testified against their friends, lovers, partners, or people widely known in the scene. None of the people I spoke to could say why they had reported on the people they did.

Most often they didn't remember doing so at all.

Matches

The second record in the dossier is "Informational Memo re: Homosexuals Implicated in Case Codename 'Matches.'" The document does not explain what the case concerned.

This is the first appearance of the author and poet Miron Białoszewski, whose name would later be invoked many times over. Apart from him, several other well-known figures are included. There is only one person the agents have doubts about; they consider the homosexuality of the remaining men "widely known."

This information interested the director of Department 2 (Counter-Espionage), who ordered them to draw up a complete "'homo' register." Apart from basic information, his greatest priority was "the basis for the allegation of perversion/the intelligence in our possession and its source." The director also asked them to "draw up separate notes for each subject or attach materials." This must be why the specific information on private individuals collected in the next three volumes was retained.

On May 29, 1962 a "List from Analysis of Homo Correspondence" was created. These documents had been sent to Department 3 (Anti-State Activities). Monitoring of the mail was a secret and therefore could not form the basis of legal proceedings. In the larger fields on this table we find suspicions about the distribution, production, or possession of pornography, which at the time was illegal. And therefore, "separately from the information garnered from reading [letters], we also obtain materials on homosexuals by confiscating documents containing pornographic photographs," wrote the report's satisfied author, before giving yet another list of names.

The premise was simple: you could find something on anyone.

"Konrad," "Stanisław," and "Grenade"

The dossiers contain reports prepared by many secret police employees, agents, informers, policemen, and denouncers. The oldest is from 1954. Its author is secret collaborator "Konrad."

He was a practical person: not interested in matters like dates of birth or even subjects' last names. Agent "Konrad" only provided useful information: where to find a given person, his profession, his possible hobbies, who his acquaintances were, and how to exploit these relationships. He also added his own observations.

"Konrad" writes, for instance, that Juliusz has recently graduated from a leathermaking vocational program, but he also attended ballet school because he had dreams of the stage. His mother recently died of tuberculosis. Juliusz is influential, though also "a man of good character." Józef is in a worse situation—a courier who left his family in the countryside and set off for Warsaw, "he behaves like a whore and having no one to look after him has derailed him completely." It's similar with Mieczysław, who despite his progressive attitude "is beginning to be dragged into the underworld of homosexuals." Janusz is a reactionary and moreover "flamboyant." Meanwhile Andrzej's homosexuality is thankfully "transitory." Unlike "Shoe" and "Ofelia," for whom all is already lost.

"Konrad" is also close to the author and poet Paweł Hertz, who grants him exceptional trust. This allows him to report that Hertz would like to spend time by the sea, preferably in Sopot, and that he also has a lover, Władek, a former policeman. At the end of his testimony, "Konrad" notes that all the information he's given dates from October 1954.

He is silent on the current situation.

Informer "Stanisław," in a hand-written note, gives his own list of homosexuals, including: a Gwardia Kraków boxer (and former Polish Socialist Party activist) as well as a Gwardia Kraków track and field athlete (a teacher from Warsaw). In addition: an actor, a writer, a professor, an employee of the Chinese Embassy, a painter, and the mysterious Puzio. He runs through several additional gay men, providing only their first names without information that could confirm their identities, for instance: Stasio from Bródno (laborer), his acquaintance F. (former major, lives in Pyry), Włodek ("a slim, frail young man in glasses"), Zbigniew (aged about twenty-one in 1954, from

Warsaw), three students at the trade school in Warsaw, and "Marek, an acquaintance of Andrzejewski's."

"Stanisław" might be happy to learn that this one acquaintance of Andrzejewski's, whose last name he was unable to confirm, was in fact the novelist's lover, Marek Keller, whom "Stanisław" no longer remembers, though finding Keller's name on the secret police list is no surprise.

The note from secret collaborator "Grenade" is short. Dr. Józef L., Dr. Włodzimierz L., and Jan M. are homosexuals. Additionally, Maciej W. is employed as a trainee journalist in a newspaper office, and Marcin C. is very interested in him. "Grenade" presumes that W. will be "yet another object of C.'s interest." Attached to the note is a list of names of "widely known" homosexuals, plus three journalists from *Ekspres Wieczorny* and *Życie Warszawy*, who are less well-known.

Cyanide in His Coffee

Gay men were very often victims of crime, including murder. They commonly committed suicide, and the dossiers contain many descriptions of such incidents.

The first is a report filed on a young man who killed himself in the bath by ingesting potassium cyanide dissolved in coffee. The dossier also states the deceased's friend was interviewed on suspicion of having murdered him. He explained the reason for his friend's suicide was deep self-hatred and the impossibility of finding a place for himself "in the outside world."

Not Only from Warsaw

The files mainly touch on Warsaw, but information was collected on homosexuals across the whole country. The majority of notes come from the southwest: Katowice, Legnica, Jelenia Góra, and Wrocław.

There is not a detailed analysis of Kraków or the Gdańsk region. These areas were considered too extensive for detailed surveillance of the "homo" phenomenon presumed to be widespread there.

Various Diseases and Oddities

On August 15, 1962, Major B. from the Counter-Espionage Department filed a report on the Warsaw homosexuals he was aware of: "In the creative, artistic, and literary community—though of course not the young people focused around the Socialist Youth Union, or Party-affiliated actors or artists—often among the older generation, there are cases of various diseases, oddities such as homosexuality, most frequently among artists: dancers and writers, often even more prominent individuals."

On Jerzy Waldorff: "A well-known music critic, art expert, author, he lives openly, cohabits with, and materially assists a dancer from the Opera named Janowski. They are widely known as a couple and there are many jokes about them. They can often be found at the club of the Polish Film and Theater Artists' Association, where Waldorff is protective of Janowski, buying him glasses of wine. This dancer is a generally effeminate type, skilled at playing women's roles onstage, e.g. the nanny in the opera *Eugene Onegin.*"

On Jarosław Iwaszkiewicz: "A leading Polish writer, has two daughters, but it is common knowledge he likes young men, and many of today's well-known writers (Paweł Hertz and others) and actors owe the beginnings of their artistic and romantic careers to Iwaszkiewicz's influence."

On Paweł Hertz: "A well-known novelist [sic], related to the well-known children's author of the same surname. The best expert on classic literature in Poland. His monographs on Słowacki are well-known. For years he has been seen with a handsome man who always accompanies him to Warsaw's cafés and bars. The man is a government employee, who is rumored to have been connected with the Ministry of Internal Affairs. I do not know his name. It would seem Paweł Hertz bears his abnormality rather tragically. He never jokes about it himself, instead he is a sorry loner."

On Jerzy Zawieyski: "Playwright. His play *The High Wall* is currently being staged at the Kameralna Theater. He was in Bulgaria this year with his 'wife' and some man who was always at their side. There have been many jokes about them, his abnormality is generally known."

The agent also described several women (he says of a well-known dancer: "a rather loose woman—that is the general opinion of her. Apparently she does not disdain living with members of either sex"), and also attempted to categorize the entire scene: "As I list a portion of those individuals I have heard of, I must add that apart from a small number of instances, this is a whole community held captive to various addictions, vodka, theft, intrigue; prostitution of men and women is a familiar phenomenon for them. The Polish Stage in particular is simply infested with the dregs of the earth, girls for hire, impresarios who trade jobs for carnal and monetary favors."

Reports

Foucault believed sexual orientation had political significance.

Homosexuality was, therefore, political.

Viewed in the right way, compiling a list of homosexuals could be the same as compiling a list of "enemies of the nation."

The reports are interlaced with crimes: murders, thefts, pedophilia. Evidence was sought of the victims' or the suspects' homosexuality. All the reports repeat the same descriptions of the community, the meeting places, the same names.

All those described are "guilty" of only one thing: homosexuality.

"Gustaw" and "Leon"

"Gustaw" is one of very few secret police authors whose memos betray no particular homophobia (as we would say today, since the term "homophobia" was not coined until 1972). His reports even show hints of sympathy. He does his best to remain objective, and is sparing in his judgments: "Homosexuality *per se* is not a dangerous phenomenon, politically or even morally. It is a natural phenomenon to the extent that the nature of some individuals inclines them to seek out intimate relations with members of the same sex."

Although "Gustaw" does not have a hostile relationship toward homosexuality, he writes that "the pederast is the same type of deviant from the general norm as the hunchback, the stutterer, or the freckle-faced. Yet while those deviances are visible, this one is hidden." He adds that, "thanks to the general cultural progression of all societies, today we no longer sneer at or persecute stutterers, hunchbacks, or redheads; with regard to homosexuals—societies' views have remained at the medieval level."

"Gustaw" discerns danger in homosexuality only when "in the event of societal condemnation; homosexuality becomes a socially active phenomenon. Like Freemasonry in former times, homosexuality remains an underground activity in all societies. Pederasts recognize each other by signs, behaviors, and means of expression that are imperceptible to normal people. Persecuted from the outside, homosexuals feel solidarity with one another (like every persecuted minority). The community of perversion connects people with adverse worldviews, seemingly creating an international, interparty mafia of persons joined by a shared, persecuted defect."

Agent "Gustaw" concludes his note by giving a few names of widely known homosexuals.

Unlike his colleague, "Leon" makes an effort in his report not so much to understand homosexuality as to seek out its origin: "Homosexuality is a familiar phenomenon in history [. . .]. There are many reasons for its occurrence. There are two theories. The first endorses an excess of hormones, e.g. estrogen in a man; the second, that the cause of homosexuality is psychological resentment, complexes arising during the period of early childhood. The weight of opinion is on the side of the former—meaning that homosexuality is an innate characteristic. Nonetheless it is indisputable that to rid oneself (as some say—cure, although the homosexual, apart from his variant interests in the sexual sphere, is a normally functioning person) of homosexuality is impossible."

"Leon" is fixated on normality. His information shows that "the majority of homosexuals most enjoy socializing with normal people; this is explained, perhaps, by the need for intimate socializing with an individual who has a clear preponderance of, e.g., masculinity in relation to the homosexual man. A second group experiences happiness in socializing exclusively with h.—seeking an individual who requires an identical experience, the same means of reaching climax. It is likely that when relations take place with a normal individual it is necessary to entice him, create proper conditions, most often with the assistance of alcohol. The normal individual feels disgust and revulsion toward the h. afterward. Here another factor in the h. plays a role—masochism or sadism. [. . .] The h.'s carnal relations are dominated by general petting, concluding in a moment of climax via mutual masturbation or oral intercourse (fellatio) in succession or simultaneously (so-called 69), while anal intercourse is only typical when one party is impotent. Nonetheless there is a widespread view of h. men that their usual technological [sic] practice is intercourse of the rectum, a view that is doubtless incorrect and without basis in practice. H. most often seek one another out in urinals, bathhouses, and railroad stations, as well as around other selected areas—cafés, public squares. [. . .] They enjoy gathering together to spend time on entertainments (particularly dancing) or at orgies.

There are annual unadvertised assemblies—in Poland, at Sopot in summer, in winter (more likely) in Zakopane.

"Psychological characteristics of h. are typical of the sex opposite to the one they formally represent. Femininity in men, the inverse in women. The typical man: soft, focused inward, on the content of his own personality and views. Fondness for more eccentric dress. Attraction to professions of a humanistic or visual character—ballet, the circus, hairdressing, tailoring (specialty: pants) [. . .]."

Clinic of Sexual Neuroses

In 1958 the psychiatrist Tadeusz Bilikiewicz published a small study on the topic of human sexuality.

In the fourth chapter of *Clinic of Sexual Neuroses* he lists all the perversions known to him:

self-violation,

narcissism,

voyeurism,

Pygmalionism,

exhibitionism,

sadism,

masochism,

taking pleasure in death,

fetishism,

attraction to minors,

attraction to the elderly,

attraction to animals,

fellatio,

licking the vulva,

licking the anus,

inserting the penis into the rectum,

transvestism,

and finally: homosexuality.

On this subject, the professor has very interesting views.

For instance, when it comes to homosexuals' choice of profession, the psychiatrist, like Agent "Leon," is of the view that they become artists, actors, filmmakers, hairdressers, waiters, and musicians.

Though homosexuality has forever been present among humans, and in Ancient Greece was even considered normal, we cannot give credence to the German scientists who say that "these deviants make up two percent of society." Such theories are exaggerations.

On the other hand, we can't be surprised by such claims, since in Berlin alone there are apparently as many as one hundred twenty cafés and bars catering to these types, and "a certain rather expensive German publication" has as many as twenty thousand readers. Pornography and general tourist licentiousness are to blame, since "big-city lupanars are often visited by those lusting after sensation and the excitable."

Homosexuals are masculine and feminine, sadistic and masochistic, show manliness or put on "women's garb." Yet the division of "perverts into an active and a passive side" is exaggerated, since these preferences usually alternate.

"The oral cavity plays the role of the vagina," while "mutually masturbatory hand motions assume the greatest significance."

True "homo" emotionality is doubtful, but if it does occur, then it is unfortunately indistinguishable from the normal kind. "Still, for the majority of homosexuals, sexual relations *per se* are a necessity to which they resort only occasionally. As with loving heterosexuals, here too a feeling of happiness arises from a spiritual bond, in a sentiment of romantic fantasy. Kisses, embraces, assurances of eternal friendship, readiness to make any sacrifice at the altar of love, the ideals of sworn brothers [. . .], all love's vows along with expressions of jealousy come together in the sentiments of homosexual lovers. [. . .] As in heterosexual love, here too the ideal of a beautiful partner motivates conscious or unconscious seeking and yearnful expectations. Whether these yearnings are satisfied is predominantly the work of happenstance, which may bring love at first sight, a state of infatuation, or years-long romantic lunacy full of the throes of passion, tragic confused feelings, acts of despair, or ecstatic outpourings."

Over half of homosexuals apparently admit attraction to young boys. "The phenomenon of homosexual prostitution is particularly despicable. Young men, often minors, fall victim to it, yielding to persuasion from adult deviants, who lure them with sweets, gifts, or money."[1] An older homosexual may also entice a youth using pictorial visualizations or possibly erotic tales, which in the case of young victims oftentimes leads to destructive masturbatory acts of a substitutionary nature, for such a boy "would surely have chosen heterosexual petting."

Luckily, Dr. Bilikiewicz declares, homosexuality can be treated, and the methods are satisfactory even among those "perverts" who are content with their deviation.

Information on the Phenomenon of Homosexuality in Poland

In the view of the Party leadership, because there were homosexuals in Poland, they could be "taken advantage of operationally."

The investigation established that there were a total of 778 homosexuals in Warsaw, Łódź, Katowice, Wrocław, and Gdańsk. At the same time, it posited this number could be several hundred times higher if the register was expanded to include other cities.

Based on data from the first 215 persons analyzed, it was determined that homosexuals were drawn most often from the intelligentsia. The largest number of men practicing homosexuality were found among actors (sixty-two), followed by officials (forty-one), writers (twenty-three), scientific and academic workers (eighteen), journalists (eight), engineers (eight), doctors (four) and lawyers (two). Forty-nine people worked in other professions.

The reports devote great attention to prostitution, which high school and college students are most frequently accused of, presumably motivated by money and professional advancement. It is suspected that homosexuals, who are frequently wealthy and influential people, create "associations" and fraternities—secret organizations supporting their members.

The report's authors note that homosexuals "recognize one another [. . .] by signs imperceptible to normal people, [. . .] they are seemingly organized in 'groups' or 'bands,' that form closed clans supporting one another." These homosexual brotherhoods and unions became an obsession of the secret police agents. The report's authors do their best to link together the surveilled men into couples and groups—according to the principle that people excluded from society create networks to serve as alternatives to family relationships.

Michel Foucault will probe an identical principle in his writings—that ostracism creates a community operating on a principle of making the abnormal into the normal.

The reports define homosexuals primarily by promiscuity, and notes that "these tendencies cause or are at the root of various types of criminal offenses, particularly murder, assault and battery, blackmail, robbery, etc." Yet most important of all is that "in isolated cases, these circumstances can also be exploited for anti-government activity."

The reports name all the bars and cafés as well as saunas and municipal bathhouses—often locations for homosexual "trysts." "Apart from these, homosexuals meet in private apartments, where so-called 'tea parties' are held, pornographic films are shown, 'balls' of various types are thrown, etc."

These homosexual "tea parties" attain mythic status among the policemen and secret collaborators assigned to "homo" cases, and the fact of having tea in the home will, in the agents' eyes, unambiguously reveal a person's sexual orientation.

The secret police focus their attention most intently on foreign contacts. Homosexuals who know foreigners, and especially those who travel outside the country, find themselves on a special list because "these people's excursions abroad may be exploited by enemy agencies."

The material gathered leads the agents to conclude that homosexuality has "tendencies to spread," therefore "it is desirable to introduce a mandatory register of homosexuals in the whole country. This register should be supplemented by data on criminal acts caused by or performed against a background of homosexuality." To this end it was essential to "establish a register of homosexuals' so-called hideouts and contact points" on a quarterly or semiannual basis.

The Code

The Criminal Code did not consider "satisfying sexual impulses contrary to nature" a crime so long as it did not occur under circumstances that were legally punishable. It delineated situations in which homosexuality might go hand in hand with criminal acts: relations with minors, rape or assault, exploitation of the disabled, abuse of a dependent relationship or exploitation of another person in distress, and also prostitution and pornography. The majority of examples collected in the files dealt with the latter two.

Article 207 of the Criminal Code: "Whoever, seeking to derive material benefit, offers himself to a person of the same sex for the purposes of an indecent act shall be subject to a penalty of imprisonment for up to three years."

This is the only regulation to mention homosexual activity.

Apart from this, anything that was not forbidden was permissible.

Officially.

People of This Category

The first volume of secret police files ends with a note on the case of "hommo" [*sic*] persons, dated October 16, 1962, which details how to further familiarize oneself with and analyze the gay community, and gives an overview of the prior reports.

Plans were made to "employ techniques of surveillance of individuals." Despite assurances that homosexuality was neither a punishable offense nor even, in fact, an excuse for surveillance, the deciding factor was the mere suspicion of homosexual behavior.

The surveillance machine was running at full steam.

"Upstanding"

Agent "Upstanding"—who started filing reports in the early '50s—infiltrated a group of Warsaw gay men, though he wasn't gay himself. He would meet with them in clubs and private spaces, memorize conversations and behavior, and then write down his observations and pass them on to the secret police.

"Regarding S. and P., I have established they are committed homosexuals, as is K., and who spend entire evenings picking up young men and performing so-called indecent acts upon them, even doing so in ruins from the war and parks. In the course of conversation, the names of dozens of homosexuals were mentioned, too many to memorize. At 5:00 P.M. I left the homosexuals' company because I could not tolerate it any longer.

"S. was speaking to R. 'about the Way of the Cross'; I asked what that meant and he answered that I was still too young. Next they talked about chapels. Laughing, I asked what that meant because once again this was all going over my head, S.

answered there was a peep show as well. Then S. explained it to me. The 'Way of the Cross' is a street where pederasts offer themselves for money. There are a few such 'Ways' in Warsaw. Meanwhile, a chapel is an apartment where pederasts live and sell themselves for money. In Warsaw, there is a peep show on Marszałkowska Street where you can view pornographic photographs and there are men on site at the customers' disposal. Entry costs 150 złotys."

In his reports, agent "Upstanding" quotes statements by homosexuals he knows. To judge from one such quote in a report filed on November 10, 1953, the target knew the community was under surveillance, saying: "A few days later they called me into the secret police [headquarters] in Mostowski Palace. Politely apologizing to me several times and asking me not to worry, they inquired whether I was homosexual. I admitted I was. They said there were 502 homosexual men in Warsaw, and opened up a large book where they had all their names."

Letter from a Young Pole

On November 6, 1962, the secret police intercepted a letter:

> Dear Sirs,
> I am a young Pole. I work for a student tourism and leisure organization and am studying in college. I receive your magazine *The Road to Friendship and Tolerance* admittedly erratically, but have always read it, for several years now. I periodically also

read the publication *Der Krieg.* I also know there are also other magazines intended for men: *L'ireadie, Virendachab.* In the past I have also had *Freund.* But my favorite is *Der Wig.*

In Poland we have no such magazines. Yet people know the biweekly magazine *Sport for All* unofficially fills in for such a publication, though publicly it serves other purposes.

It is also universally known that Poland is a country where, on the one hand the birth rate is high—which in the view of sociological experts is becoming a certain problem in our post-war conditions—while on the other hand it is a country with a relatively significant number of men interested in practicing homosexuality, who think that: "with women you can have a baby, but you can achieve love and happiness only in a relationship with another man."

In Poland, there are a few larger urban areas where homosexuals are an entirely normal phenomenon, where the public does not even find them surprising. You must know it is not Poland's legal regulations but the backwardness of public opinion that is the element prompting our male sex not to reveal themselves.

In Poland, the question of sexual intercourse is from the youngest age considered a private matter for each individual. The law does not interfere in these matters. Since 1932 there has been only one legal regulation in the Code of Criminal Conduct—article 207—stating sexual intercourse with a person of the same sex is punishable if performed only with the intention of deriving material benefit. Of course there are cases, particularly in larger cities such as Kraków, Warsaw, Katowice, Gdynia, etc., where some young men wish to profit from these types of friendships or acquaintances. But generally speaking, Poland is a country where acquaintances of this type are formed quickly and generously.

There are very many of us homophiles. No government or police authority is interested in us or interferes in our affairs. We do not belong to any organization or association. Nor do we have any clubs, as is the case in Western Europe. We meet only in cafés, of which there are a large number in Poland, in student clubs, in dormitory buildings, in private apartments, in well-known health resorts, and last of all in bathhouses. We know that in Western Europe and in America there are many publications targeted toward men. Yet such books or magazines reach us irregularly. The censors do not confiscate this type of literature and photography if they arrive in small numbers. Nor do we pay any customs duties. Yet what we get is a proverbial drop in the ocean.

We are unable to subscribe to these publications because we have no foreign currency with which to do so. From time to time, various illustrated publications appear here, such as *Photographing the Nude, Love in the Art of Photography, Beauty and Strength in Sport*.

Of the books targeted toward us, we have had local editions of *Wenn das Korn nicht gestorbt* by Andre Gilde,[2] *Naked Man* by Gregor Timofiejew[3] and perhaps the most successful Polish publication, *The Doors of Paradise* by Jerzy Andrzejewski.[4] But that is all, and is still too little.

I read your magazine with fascination, and the attached pictures are truly a welcome sight. I am writing so that you know your publication also reaches Poland, where it finds many enthusiasts and is greeted with joy.

This young Pole's enthusiasm did not reflect reality.

The letter, published in the pamphlet *The Path to Friendship and Tolerance* (*Der Weg zu Freundschaft und Toleranz*), is located in the archives of the Institute of National Remembrance. This small newsletter looks like a cheap high-school publication. It's less than twenty pages long, and attached to it are photographs of posing bodybuilders.

None show complete nudity.

An Interesting Person

One of the people described in the files is Włodek Ch.

He was a minor con man and petty thief. According to police notes he'd been arrested three times for stealing items of clothing and food.

Yet there was something that set Włodek apart from the thieves and other wheeler-dealers. On one of the lists of homosexuals, comprising fifty-seven names (of professors, editors, priests, one actor, one store manager, one waiter, and one mineworker), only Włodek has an annotation stating this person "is interesting."

We don't know if Włodek started snitching out of fear and envy, or for pleasure and praise. Nor do we know if the officers obtained his confessions—typed and also handwritten, in nearly calligraphic script full of flourishes and bulges, underlines, exclamation marks, and run-on sentences—by force or through polite conversation. One thing is certain: Włodek knew a lot and eagerly shared his knowledge.

Trailing Włodek was agent "Marek," who quickly became

an important figure for this gay secret collaborator. The correspondence between these men, conducted in 1963, gives a sense of shared sympathy. Włodek wrote long, fiery letters to "Marek," with denunciations included seemingly as an afterthought. The replies have not survived.

For instance, Włodek reported that "on May 6 of this year at the Polonia café, there was a conference of homosexuals from all over Poland. At this conference they discussed the issue of communication between homosexuals in different cities and other organizational matters." During this period Włodek submitted statements on over fifty homosexuals, mainly from Warsaw, Kraków, Silesia, and Zakopane. He most often gave full personal details, including place of residence, occupation, financial status, and of course a short annotation: homosexual, bisexual, queer, homo. If he wasn't sure of someone's name, he gave an approximate description of their physical and facial features, including information about preferences and places where the person in question normally spent their time. He added handwritten notes to these testimonies, underlined the most important information, and listed interesting pseudonyms.

From Włodek's Reports

First on the list is Tomasz M., former vacation-house manager and a bisexual, who can often be seen in Katowice, Bytom, Zabrze, or Chorzów "owing to the convenient streetcar connections." Włodek met him in one of the Silesian cities, at the apartment of a former priest named Franciszek. Both

Father Franciszek and Tomasz M. live together with a certain Mirosław. In addition to this, Tomasz M.—a divorcé with two daughters—keeps "lovers, despite not loving them effusively and the fact that they most often abandon him." He sleeps with young men in the vacation houses he manages. From day-to-day he lives with a woman who, "when he is unemployed, supports him as well as his lovers," with money she made by selling off property she owned. In this family "Tomasz M.'s spending sets off scenes of pandemonium."

Next is Stefan R.: "secretive to the limits of decency" and married, so "he doesn't go around publicly."

Józef—an amateur double bassist—rarely goes to bed with men and needs no money because he is wealthy. He whiles the time away playing music for himself, his wife, and his boys.

Money is also not a problem for Władysław W., a waiter at the Orbis on Gubałówka Mountain, outside Zakopane. He left his wife and that is why he meets up with young men. Włodek proudly remarks they had fun every day in the hotels. "NB: the majority of young waiters sleep around, and very intensively at that!"

Stanisław P., a former Party activist, had to abandon his hometown in exchange for his "communism *par excellence*." He lives in Warsaw, where he is often beaten up because he likes picking up men in the area around Three Crosses Square. In Włodek's view, the young man "is, frankly, embarrassing himself" and doesn't appreciate the comfortable position he's attained, thanks to a promotion to the Propaganda Department of the Party's Central Committee. And it's a shame, because "he displays profound intelligence and an education that one might say goes beyond surface-level," though simultaneously he has an "unremarkable appearance" and "a great fondness for the erotic."

One priest, Jakub W., prefers striking up acquaintances at the city baths in Katowice. "He absolutely wants a boyfriend—he is committed to financing one." He requires total discretion, and so, for instance, receives correspondence at P.O. Box 44 in the city. "Not erotically choosy, given he got to know Mirosław M. in the bathhouse." He has to support his mentally ill mother. He also supports some young man, who, he stubbornly insists, is not his lover. He makes the rounds of the cafés in civilian garb.

The "clerical homosexual" officially most well-known on a national scale is Father Stanisław W. Educated in Kraków, this "son of a petty farmer entered the ministry to have a better life." At home, "in the presbytery he hosts such queers as" Mieczysław Z. and Tadeusz S., who "insult him to his face as a pimp and a bastard." He often comes to Kraków for so-called guest appearances, when he frequently "whores around in his cassock, though most often in plainclothes." He squanders money heedlessly, "sleeps around with street thugs and soldiers, so-called Little Red Riding Hoods, for whom he buys vodka or to whom he gives money." He is very popular and can be seen in many places, such as the Kaprys nightclub. He never misses any of the sex parties thrown by Stanisław J., "a dealer in foreign currency, though officially in vegetables," better known by his stage name "Queen Barbara Radziwiłł," and who, Włodek has heard, was "awarded the Order of the Great Cunt for services to Polish pederasty." Father Stanisław is also notorious for officiating the marriage of a certain Zbyszek from Rabka to his lover in the commandos.

The journalist Ryszard O., as a bisexual, meets men very discreetly, has sexual relations with them, but "doesn't flaunt his practices." He works in television and has a grandly and very expensively furnished apartment, where Włodek has spent time along with an elegant and very intelligent friend, a prostitute named Anna. The journalist goes out with women, but doesn't refrain from homosexual adventures and can often be found at the cocktail bar in the Hotel Francuski and at the Warszawianka café.

(Anna the prostitute, the only woman Włodek goes into detail about, is married and often spends time in Warsaw, where "she earns good money among habitual gamblers and hosts an elegant, underground roulette den." She herself sometimes plays, though "she has a den of prostitutes in Kraków that mainly supports her." The brothel is located in her home, meaning the apartment of her "fat and remarkably lecherous" husband. Anna herself is a tall, very handsome woman with "literally demonic eyes.")

A Kraków secret police officer and *éminence grise* of the ordinary police, Zdzisław R., "has houseboys/lovers, because he is very well off," and often hosts uniformed policemen for sex, at which times he'll throw a drinking party for a larger group.

"The determined homosexual Piotr M." lives in Jaszczurówka and is a romantic. He would like anyone he loves to be utterly and exclusively devoted to him. He earns an average salary, but nevertheless spares no expense on his meetings with men, whose "culmination is erotica and everlasting love." This romantic would "tell you his greatest sin, as well as a trifle like the code names from military headquarters, which he constantly rattles off." And: "He smokes moderately, drinks little."

Lech S. is a young man, about twenty-two years old, a slim blond of average height and in a gray suit. But most of all he's "a queer, a pimp, and a prostitute." He always hangs out at the Alhambra.

Andrzej D. is a bisexual who runs a sporting goods shop, meaning he "can take the liberty of closing his store every day at about eleven and receive his young lovers during that time." They can then make love in the office "on government furniture." The store owner "does not go out publicly and avoids the homosexual clan's cafés." Yet he adores the Roman baths, and it was at one of these, on Nowy Świat, that Włodek met him. Włodek acknowledges "he is very attractive as a man and lover, polite, elegant, and really very kind. Active."

One mysterious and dangerous-sounding note is on Stanisław, who lives in Wołomin. In the informer's opinion, Stanisław is "a graveyard jackal, a common queer, a bum who lives off of stealing flowers in the cemetery and selling them to his florist grandmother, Czesława."

Another "common queer" is Zbigniew P.—"all in all, nothing interesting."

Józef Ż. is "queer/married." He maintains a good relationship with the Ministry of Internal Affairs and has a son being raised by a female relative in Wrocław. "Knows the ins and outs of his bustling trade in sweaters made of cotton from unraveling socks at a price of less than twenty złotys." Apart from this he is "active in sleeping with men, and sentimental." At times he "is driven to tears by being too unsure of someone's feelings."

Andrzej T. is "crazy in bed." He's a handsome actor and a married bisexual, whom Włodek met at the Cyganeria restaurant in Kraków.

In Silesia, Włodek met a certain Arkadiusz, who, "as a male prostitute and simultaneously a thief supporting young men financially, has luck with both women and men."

Jan J. is plagued by endless financial problems. He lives in Zakopane with his wife, who has a respiratory illness and knows about his homosexual inclinations. J. often picks fights and ends up in jail, but his friend, a homosexual police sergeant, can always spring him. Afterward they go drinking together, and the lottery kiosk that J. runs in Krupówki falls into neglect.

The surgeon Andrzej L. is supplied boys by his friend Ika, "a thrice-married—and once a countess by marriage—drunk, advanced consumptive, and occasional discreet prostitute."

Professor Jerzy K. is married and has adult sons. "Bisex." Also: alcoholic. "His wife calls him a pederast and impotent" but it doesn't bother him. He's an elegant, very handsome, athletic older man. "A huge pushover."

Zbigniew C., whose name is underlined in red, is a "determined homosexual," and his mother works in the United States Embassy. Zbigniew "only likes youthful bodies and is active." Beyond that, he was arrested by the police during the political upheaval of October 1956 for brandishing an anti-government slogan. He is independently wealthy. "In terms of hobbies, he's interested in photography."

Włodek met Zbyszek C. in the company of Henryk the Countess, Michel Foucault's friend. Zbyszek C. has since passed away, but the photographs he took of young men are truly very beautiful.

Unfortunately, Foucault is not in any of them.

Memo on Foucault

Dossier 1, pages 63–64 (names underlined in red):

Warsaw, Aug 9, 1962 (confidential)

List of persons suspected of sexual deviancy.

1. P., René [. . .] French cit.—secretary archivist of the French Embassy in Warsaw, is probably homosexual. Indicated by agency information from sources "Flight," "Janek," "General." The aforementioned sources state P. behaved unnaturally toward them, admiring their figures, attempting to grope their hips, knees, and genitals, as well as unambiguously proposed "some fun together" in his apartment.

2. J., Christian [. . .] French cit., former French teacher at Jagiellonian University. In April 1962 departed permanently for France. We have photographic material evidence proving J. is a homosexual.

3. Ś., Waldemar [. . .] Polish cit., 3rd yr student, Main School of Planning and Statistics, res. in Warsaw [. . .]. Stated during operational conversation that [he] is a homosexual. Ś. has maintained sexual relations with the following:

– Foucault, Michael, French cit., former French lecturer at UW, resident during his stay in Poland in Warsaw at 37 Rutkowski St[5] apt 27. Departed for Paris in 1960, where he is said to remain to the present day.

– R., Henryk, columnist. Has also spent time at Foucault's apartment.

– F., Mirosław, novice theater artist, former member of Mazowsze ensemble. Has also spent time at Foucault's apartment.

– O., Stefan, clerk at an international trade depot. Has also spent time at Foucault's apartment.

Sr. Ops. Off. Div. 8 Dept. 2

Terakowski, H. (Maj.)

> [I]n a general manner
> madness [. . .] is not linked to the world and its subterranean forms
> but rather to man and his frailties, his dreams and illusions.
>
> *History of Madness*

FOUCAULT'S MADNESS
(WARSAW)

1958

Warsaw had a population of 1.83 million people (in 1939: 1.3 million, in 1945: 1.62 million).

A fifth bridge across the Vistula was under construction, near the Citadel. The Warsaw Stadium train station had been completed. In Wola and Bielany districts, apartment buildings were rising amid the meadows. Reconstructed historic buildings, colorful as toy blocks, were springing up on Zamkowy Square. The scaffolding had come down from the Wielki Theater. Across the river, Saska Kępa district was extending southward. The apartments there had red balconies, and people came to get a look at the cheery sight. Garages were being built near homes and apartment buildings—the thought people might own personal cars was astounding.

The Warsaw night glowed with neon signs: over the Ruch news kiosk by the Polonia Theater, or the Stefan Żeromski

Bookstore, at Radio Telewizja electronics in Muranów district, and, soon, at GalSkór leather goods. Colorful nocturnal symbols in green, red, and yellow, like traffic lights.

Scattered here and there were police booths and phone booths. The latter were so popular you had to wait in line to make a call. There was a certain phone booth etiquette in place. You had to let your companions in line know if your conversation was going to run long. Rapping on the window was acceptable.

The police booths were very narrow, and their roofs bore a neon sign with the police force's initials. They looked exactly like the phone booths, except inside stood a policeman with a whistle and a cap, prepared to intervene in an emergency.

The two-level self-service restaurant on the corner of Świętokrzyska and Czacki Streets offered 120 standing places on the first floor and one hundred on the second. There was also seating upstairs. The citizens of Warsaw would stop by for a cigarette, a small coffee, and a pastry. They would stand around little tables. The floor was a mosaic of small black-and-white tiles.

Some claim it was much more common to go for a large shot of vodka before work than after. In the evenings you'd drink at home, with your family. Statistics showed the typical citizen of Warsaw consumed one egg, one pastry, and 1.5 quarter-liter bottles of vodka per week. There was a ban on selling alcohol to intoxicated persons, minors, at outdoor markets, or in late-night stores (this prohibition was ignored).

Every day Warsaw's citizens drank 280,000 liters of milk, 25,000 liters of vodka, and twice as much wine (beer was not recorded).

Every day eighty people ended up in the drunk tank, including eight women. In September alone, police cars were called out for domestic disputes exactly 1,488 times. Ambulances were called over eight thousand times.

Przekrój magazine reported the threat of inflation had been headed off, and the market was saturated with consumer goods. "In theory," government-set prices would not go up, and if they did, it would be made up for by reductions in the prices of alternative goods. For instance: a rise in the price of veal led to a reduction in the price of rubber-soled shoes.

The average Warsaw citizen earned one thousand złotys a month or more. Pensions and salaries for textile and paper manufacturing workers had risen.

The fifth volume of *In Search of Lost Time* by Marcel Proust, titled *The Prisoner*, had just come out in Polish, the latest translation from the pen of the renowned Tadeusz Boy-Żeleński.

Kraków's Wawel Cathedral celebrated the first consecration of a bishop in thirty years, with *Przekrój* reporting he was a "a very young and modern sportsman, the Reverend Prof. Karol Wojtyła."

The Moskwa Cinema was showing *Eroica* and *Moulin Rouge*. Others were also showing *Ashes and Diamonds*, which people waited in lines half a kilometer long to see. The usher would mark entry tickets with a pen, never pencil, so no one could take an eraser to them and resell them.

Men slicked their hair back. They wore berets with tabs on top.

Women hunted for the widely-advertised "horseshoe" skirts from Dior. But they were nowhere to be found.

There were true wonders on sale in the private shopping pavilions on Marszałkowska Street. That is where, for
instance, a young lady named Małgosia first saw a blouse made
of synthetic material. Dark pink. What a shock! Małgosia
remembers her surprise to this day, because she'd never seen
such a color with her own eyes before. Supposedly it had
existed before the war, but not since.

An ad for the popular weekly declared: "Buy your wife *Przekrój*—it will keep her busy for 114 minutes!"

In the magazine's view, a woman should be like a kitten,
and the ideal wife worried when her husband was late coming
home from work, but never let her concern show. She would
also never complain of being tired or compare her labor to
his. Instead, she would be well dressed and coiffed, serve him
his favorite food for dinner, and not reproach him for bringing friends home unannounced. Before her husband left the
house, the ideal wife should give him a sincere, but not soppy,
kiss. In the evening she would let him relax and listen to the
game on the radio, even if at that very moment her favorite
songs were playing on the other station. While a wife bustled
around the kitchen and took care of the house, her husband
would read the papers. If her husband was a competent head
of household, he knew laundering a men's suit cost fifty złotys
and a shirt, five złotys; that lunch for four people required a
kilo of potatoes; and also that there were two types of butter:
blue and red (and the latter was more expensive). That was all
a man really needed to know, because for everything else, he
had his wife.

Przekrój also reported on a statistical analysis of one thousand citizens surveyed in provincial sexual health clinics.

About forty percent of women and forty-eight percent of men stated they became sexually active between the ages of eighteen and twenty, while sixty-five percent declared they make no use of prostitutes.

A Warsaw taxi driver named B. had been murdered. Someone shot him in the back of the head. He was twenty-four. On the day of his funeral, a procession of several hundred taxis followed the coffin down Marszałkowska Street. People stood at attention on the sidewalks.

A photograph had been found of Anne Frank at age eleven, causing people to once again reflect on the depths humankind can sink to.

The First Days

Michel Foucault's stay in Poland, as with any foreigner, was important for the intelligence services, but perhaps not as important as the very moment he crossed the border into the country, and when he would eventually leave. He was only allowed in through the border crossing specified on his visa and at the specific date indicated. He could depart at that same place or potentially elsewhere, so long as the change of location was justified.

After his arrival, Foucault had twenty-four hours to register · at a district office, police station, or hotel.

He was allowed to bring:

Outerwear, underwear, shoes, toiletries, comforters, and pillows (if these added up to no more than half a kilo in weight)—without restriction;

a camera—only with 16 mm film (no more than five rolls);

a handgun (and twenty-five bullets)—or a rifle if he intended to hunt (and one hundred cartridges);

and as much medicine as his stay required.

He was not allowed to import gold, platinum, precious gems, or pearls into Poland if their weight exceeded fifty grams.

The boys explained to Michel Foucault that chocolate, coffee, tea, and especially vodka were practically currency in the People's Republic. The first time he came into Poland the customs guard informed him he was permitted to bring up to six kilos of food products, including:

1 kilo of chocolate,

250 grams of mushrooms,

200 grams of coffee,

200 grams of tea,

and 100 grams of spices.

Every time he crossed the Polish border after that, he brought hard-to-get items—including pamphlets—and when the boys were on their way to pick him up from the airport, they'd wonder who'd get what.

Foucault didn't have much of a taste for alcohol at the time, but he took it on faith that in Poland everything could be sorted out either with its help or in its presence. The same with cigarettes. For a pack of Marlboros you could speed up a home renovation, get anywhere in a taxi, or ingratiate yourself with officials. Foucault could bring ten packets of cigarettes over the border (or, alternatively, fifty cigars or two hundred and fifty grams of tobacco).

He didn't bring vodka—they had that there. It was available without restriction.

"The value of the goods you import to Poland may not exceed fifteen hundred Polish złotys. You may not sell these goods in People's Poland," the customs officer may have said.

"Of course, I don't intend to sell anything. What about books?" Foucault would have asked.

"Allowed, if they're not banned ones."

Foucault's Warsaw apartment had no books. Nor did he spend time in the library. He would often borrow a title from Professor Leszek Kołakowski of the Polish Academy of Sciences. If he was looking for newspapers or literature in French, he had to go to the International Press and Book Club—the only place you could read foreign-language publications. The Club sold newspapers from twenty-nine countries. It organized events with authors and journalists, hosted themed or discussion events, and offered foreign-language courses. There you might find an interesting exhibition of photography or contemporary painting.

Or meet someone.

Foucault filled out the border control paperwork while still in Sweden, at the Polish consulate in Stockholm at 35 Karlavägan; he attached two current photos, paid seven dollars, and was ready to leave.

His passport has survived to this day, though the photo has been torn out.

Initially he stayed in the Hotel Bristol on Krakowskie Przedmieście. We know this from Foucault himself—who told Bernard Kouchner, co-founder of Médecins du Monde, during a visit to Warsaw in 1982—and also from a letter he wrote to a friend back in 1958, in which he mentioned he was staying in a "socialist palace."

The director of the Center for French Culture, admittedly not yet known as a great philosopher but who doubtless stood out amid the gray of the post-Stalinist years, must have attracted attention at the hotel.

Was he treated as a special guest?

A young Frenchman with a sophisticated Western gentility and a bulging wallet must have riveted people's attention.

We don't know in what room, on what floor, or for how long Foucault stayed at the Bristol. No one remembers anything and the archives, including the guest list, have vanished.

Foucault liked taking walks.

Just behind the Hotel Bristol, there was a small pool in front of the Viceregal Palace—on the spot where the monument to Prince Józef Poniatowski now stands—where Foucault might have stopped by on hot days. Across the street, the Potocki Palace housed the Ministry of Culture and Art. Luxury cars would park in front of the Bristol. A wide awning hung over the entrance and tables would be put out in summer.

The Hotel Bristol café supposedly had the best pastries in the city, and in the evenings there was a dance club and cabaret. The summer sidewalk terrace was surrounded by a metal barrier decorated with potted palms. Umbrellas over the tables shaded guests from the sun. People chatted and smoked cigarettes in holders made of glass or wood.

Foucault would sit in the shade and write.

He would drink coffee and smoke.

He would read the paper.

Is that really what he did? We don't know. Daniel Defert thinks it wasn't Foucault's habit to sit among people in a café on the street and write. Maybe he ate at the hotel restaurant, but given it was fall, the image of Foucault writing in the outside café is more likely a fantasy.

"Well, unless it was cold in the room, and like Sartre in his time, Foucault preferred to work and warm himself up at the same time at a café table," adds Defert, who thinks the Bristol's terrace could have been heated.

Orbis

The Bristol belonged to the Orbis travel agency. Foucault would have been able to see the enormous globe glowing in blue neon atop the agency's building at the corner of Bracka Street and Jerozolimskie Avenue. Maybe it was a point of reference for him, a landmark for the nearby Roxana and Alhambra cafés.

The Orbis at 16 Bracka Street was the largest and oldest travel agency in Poland, operating since 1925. This was the only agency in Poland that could reserve a room in any hotel, book any kind of ticket for any airline in the world or for domestic or international trains. It was also a place where a traveler could exchange money, rent a car, or book tickets for the theater or an organized tour. There were also advertisements in English for vacations at "holiday-resorts or sanitoriums," as well as hunting or fishing trips to choose from. These latter amusements were fairly affordable. To kill a wolf: ten dollars, a fox: fifty dollars, and a wild duck: fifty cents. The most expensive trophy animal was a lynx—to shoot a single animal cost 460 dollars.

It was a little tricky with dollars: they were used as a standard for currency conversion, but no one knew how much they were worth. *Przekrój* laid out the problem: "According to the official international exchange rate, [one dollar is worth] four złotys. Yet if a foreigner brought some and exchanged them at the Polish National Bank at the special rate, they would be worth twenty-four złotys apiece. If he received them by wire from relatives and cashed them in at the PKO Bank via Gallus, today they would be worth eighty-six złotys apiece. If at that same PKO Bank he bought some attractive commodity and then sold it, then they might be worth over one hundred złotys apiece, though admittedly on the black market. If I were a certain peasant woman from near Końskie, that same dollar would have no value to me, because I wouldn't know if it was legal tender! It would sit at the bottom of a box along with some paper rubles with the portrait of Tsar Nicholas on them—something that really happened recently!"[6]

Foreign tourists enjoyed staying at Orbis hotels, so these were staked out by informers and the intelligence services. The secret police had all visitors from abroad investigated. They also investigated the people doing the investigating. If a hotel staff member managed to get to know a guest and started informing on them, the secret police would open a file on that staff member too. From the bellhop to the concierge to the elevator operator—anyone could be an informant and anyone could have a file.

For that matter, so could taxi drivers, ticket agents, airline stewards, and dining-car waiters.

In particular cases where the secret police considered it worthwhile, a bugging device would be installed or activated in a hotel room. Collected in the archives is a description of the network of these bugs, along with room and building floor plans. It is a true map of wiretapped Warsaw—and the most important location on it is the Bristol Hotel.

The secret police dossiers on Orbis include surveillance plans as well as extensive lists of informers and their targets.

Foucault is not among them.

He himself quickly realized he was being watched, but he ignored it. Defert tells me that for many years to come, Foucault recalled the fascinating absurdity of the system. He was aware someone was following him. His Polish friends warned him to not trust the hotel staff or the waiters, and especially not to bring back any boys he met. It seems to a certain extent Foucault neglected their advice, that he wasn't afraid or maybe even chose to expose himself. The boys told me he wasn't careful, he was very frank, trusting, and uninhibited in conversation. He shared the things he had and he didn't hide who he was.

This was the world he was living in, and such a world— even if it was mad, or maybe precisely because it was mad— fascinated Foucault and inspired him to work on his doctoral thesis. That, after all, was the most important thing.

Spending Money

Because Foucault was authorized for a long-term stay, he was permitted to make one-way currency exchanges: foreign currency for złotys. When he was leaving Sweden, Foucault still had a few kronor and, of course, French francs on him. According to the official rate, one hundred francs would get him 487.38 zł, and one hundred Swedish kronor—462.14 zł. The Orbis exchange counters in Warsaw were located at the airport and in the most important hotels. The National Bank of Poland, where Foucault initially exchanged his money, had branches on Karowa, Nowogrodzka, and Jasna Streets. Foucault quickly realized he would find a better rate on the black market, though doing so was a complicated matter.

So maybe that is why the Countess's friend Jurek was so close to Foucault?

Jurek knew Warsaw street life like no other.

The Center for French Culture paid Foucault in złotys. He wasn't allowed to convert the złotys or take them out of the country, but it was hard to spend everything locally. So he would eat in the finest restaurants and always treat his guests, but he still found himself with money left over. He had no taste for luxury and didn't like to show off or make a fuss about himself; for instance, he might order lunch every day in the popular and unpretentious Bar Zdrojowy. If he felt like some Jewish cuisine, he could have gone to Samson at 3 Freta Street. In the milk bars—cheap canteen-style restaurants where he went with his Polish friends—tomato soup with rice cost 8.50 zł; bean soup with potatoes, 10.60 zł; and top-quality potato dumplings and fatback, 24.70 zł. However, meat shortages on the market meant some Poles at this time were vegetarian—as was Foucault.

But sometimes there was luxury to be found. For some decent coffee, cake or ice cream, Foucault might have made his way to one of the five cafés run by the Warsaw Gastronomic Institutes: the Sejmowa (2 Górnośląska Street), the

Ujazdowska (47 Ujazdowskie Avenue), the Mirowska (4 Solna Street, no. 16), the Alhambra (32 Jerozolimskie Avenue), or the Roxana (34 Jerozolimskie Avenue). Just off Świętokrzyska Street, there was a small store catering to foreigners and those with foreign currency. People called it "behind the yellow-lace curtains"—since you couldn't see inside from the street. Foucault could purchase luxury goods there without restriction.

He did his everyday shopping at Delikatesy grocery stores, for instance at 53 Nowy Świat or 33 Wilcza Street. At these— especially the one on Wilcza, which was open twenty-four hours—a person could buy whatever they wanted or order delivery to their home, even by phone. An advertisement declared in English: "Remember! Day-and-Night Service Delikatesy. Your gift will be delivered by special Messenger at the given place, on the given day, at the given hour." The store offered coffee, tea (options: Ceylon, Chinese, Indian), olives, sardines, fruit juices, wines (from Bulgaria, France, Armenia, and Hungary), champagne, brandy, rum, cigarettes, and fine vodka. All this was exclusively for so-called foreign currency customers.

A man does not live by food alone. Fortunately for Foucault, cultural entertainment was not expensive either: the theater cost 8–30 złotys a ticket, the opera: 12–45, the operetta: 10–35, the orchestra: 6–25, and the movies, only 4–15. So Foucault found himself throwing money around left and right. Yet today his home in Paris does not contain a single object, book, or even the tiniest napkin that might have been brought from Poland. Nothing he purchased could be taken out of the country.

The best way of getting rid of złotys was simply to give them to someone. And Foucault was happy to do so.

According to Nuda

On the matter of homosexuality, Nuda (whose nickname means "boring") has conservative views. He thinks his own homosexuality was caused by his absent father. How does Nuda know? From his family history, as well as ones similar to his—which are too numerous to count.

As far as what comes first: the man or his homosexuality, Nuda is absolutely convinced it is the man, and he would have us believe affection is secondary and culturally conditioned. After all, homosexuality is not natural, according to Nuda, whose real name is Bogusław and who knows everything about the Warsaw of those days: how people did it, where they did it, and especially—for what price.

Casting his mind back, he says for one hundred dollars Foucault would have had no trouble getting acquainted with five soldiers from the honor guard, having dinner with them at the Bristol, drinking the finest vodka, eating mountains of the best kiełbasa, dancing the night away, and then, in the morning, discreetly letting each soldier out of his room, slipping a small tip into each man's pocket for his girlfriend. That tip might be, for instance, one American dollar, meaning about twenty-five złotys (at the National Bank) or even one hundred złotys (on the street). At the street rate, a Pole earned about twenty-five dollars a month; at the bank rate—one hundred dollars.

What soldier wouldn't?

That one night was worth as much as a month's salary.

Travels

Meanwhile, Foucault had only just settled down in Warsaw.

He was getting to know the city, its people, and his job. He probably missed his friends from Sweden and Paris. It's true that he could travel from Warsaw to many European cities by train, but it appears over his time in Poland he rarely left the country.

He definitely went to the funeral of his father, who died on September 14, 1959. The time the boys picked him up from the airport was in early summer 1959, but that couldn't have been his first time arriving in Poland, because he already knew Stefan and the Countess.

He definitely went to Gdańsk and Kraków to lecture on Apollinaire. The text of his lecture is a few small handwritten pages. Foucault's handwriting is even and decisive, the individual lines of text are broadly spaced, as if to leave room for potential edits—though Foucault, unlike Proust, only made rare and brief additions in the margins. He attached no great weight to the lecture, but when he left Poland, he brought it home with him—possibly the only item he took. To this day it has not been published.

Given the subject of his research, he made inquiries about a hospital for those with mental disorders, and was recommended to visit Tworki, the famous psychiatric facility outside Warsaw. Yet no one knows whether Foucault ever actually went; the hospital archives make no mention of him. It's similar with the Auschwitz–Birkenau concentration camp: Foucault definitely went there on his third trip to Poland, but even during his first he probably could have visited the camp while staying in Kraków. Yet the museum's documentation is silent on the subject.

Did he go back to Stockholm?

Foucault could have reached Stockholm by train, via Berlin and Malmö. He'd spent over two years in Sweden and left behind many close friends. His address book from this period is overflowing with Swedish names. There are also a few Polish ones.

Did he go to Paris?

A train ran every day from Warsaw to Paris, passing through either Prague (2,021 kilometers) or Berlin (1,684 kilometers). If Foucault chose the Prague route, he'd pay 230.10 zł for first class or 154.15 zł for coach. If—as is more likely—he went through Berlin, he'd pay 197.25 zł for first class and 132.85 zł for coach. So the Berlin route was most reasonable—cheaper, faster, and in an Orbis sleeping car.

The express train covered the distance from the Polish border to Berlin in ninety minutes to two hours. For comparison, a train from Poland to Moscow took nineteen hours; to Stockholm, twenty-three hours and thirty minutes; and to Paris, a whole twenty-four hours. Passing through Berlin, at the time divided by the Wall, meant crossing a literal boundary between worlds: East and West. That boundary symbolized the struggle between light and darkness. The train station in East Berlin was dark and deserted. The Western station was packed with people, and new arrivals were greeted by a huge blue-and-white advertisement for the Bayer company.

The most popular option was to travel by sleeper train. The cost of a prix fixe breakfast or lunch in the dining car ranged from 20 to 30 złotys, or 15–25 złotys per dish à la carte. You could sip a cocktail and light up a cigarette. Express trains, which had no dining car, often had a cold buffet and hors d'œuvres, as well as vodka and beer. These trains were also staked out by informers.

Secret collaborator "Kostek" reported from the sleeper train to Stockholm: "S. is somewhat odd. When talking about women he expresses disgust. He says intimate relations with women don't appeal to him at all, they give him no pleasure. He admits his desire to love a man. For instance, while talking to his friend, he repeatedly cuddled up against him and stroked his face, saying: you good fellow. He behaved in a similar way toward me. S. has a Swiss watch costing 235 marks. Where from? Not from work, to be sure."

Perhaps floating around somewhere is a report naming sleeper-train passenger Michel Foucault.

Other Possibilities

Foucault mainly got around Warsaw on foot.

The University, the Center for French Culture, his apartment, as well as all the places of leisure he frequented were close to one another. Yet if he happened to take public transit, he could buy a ticket for the streetcar for fifty groszy or for the bus for eighty groszy. The bulky, red, barrel-shaped 54 trolley-bus ran down Krakowskie Przedmieście, so he could hop on it at the Amatorska café and get off at the University. Sometimes, when he had business outside the City Center, he might take a taxi: four złotys for the first kilometer and two złotys for each subsequent one. At night the rate was fifty percent higher. For thirty złotys an hour, the driver would stick around with the meter running.

Foucault enjoyed driving, so maybe he drove to Poland in his legendary beige Jaguar sports car. He definitely drove it around Sweden, and also to France before he moved to Warsaw. If he did, he'd have had to enter the country through the port of Gdynia.

"Have they got good roads in Poland?" Foucault might have asked.

"Sure do, sir, sure do," someone would have answered. "If they're there, they're good."

While living in Warsaw, there are a few things Foucault would have learned quickly:

— the museums were closed on Mondays and days immediately following a holiday;

— theater and movie tickets for Saturday or Sunday had to be purchased three days in advance;

— churches were open to visitors between 9 A.M. and 5 P.M.;

— the streetcars, buses, and trolleybuses were the most crowded between 3 P.M. and 5 P.M. (during this time it was also hard to find an open table at a restaurant);

— street numbers ran according to the flow of the Vistula River;

— finding parking was not especially difficult, but there was only one guarded lot, on the Old Town's market square (which was not yet pedestrianized);

— restaurants were open until 10 P.M., dance clubs until 3 A.M.; at Category S (super) and Category 1 (first-class) restaurants, breakfast cost 15–20 złotys, lunch 30–50 złotys, and dinner 30–50 złotys (Category 1 was higher than S);

— at dance clubs it was required to spend, depending on the class of venue, a minimum of 60–100 złotys (you had to buy an appropriate voucher, with the price starting at exactly sixty złotys).

The Palace

The monster, the largest construction site, the graveyard of Warsaw, a monument to hubris, and a concrete hulk of no use to anybody.

A Soviet-built skyscraper, a permanent symbol of authority and control.

Today, a symbol of Warsaw: the Palace of Culture and Science.

In a well-known color photograph from 1958, the Palace stands at the center of a square surrounded by rubble, ruins, grass, and thickets. It's completely white, like some funeral monument made of Hawaiian beach sand. It pierces the sky. At its top, a spire protrudes from an enormous sphere. An unknown poet wrote of it: "The wind atop the Palace roars with all its might / On high, a crystal bauble glistens in the light."[7] The Palace is monumental and overwhelming. It is like a city within the city. The Great Cathedral. Kafka's castle. The eye of Sauron and the Panopticon.

What did Foucault think of the Palace?

He would certainly have found it interesting. When a few years later he came up with his idea of a guard tower controlling everything around it with an unseeing eye, perhaps it would resemble the Palace of Culture in Warsaw.

After all, from his apartment at the end of Rutkowski Street, he saw it every day.

The Center

The "Warsaw Sorbonne," meaning the Institut Français,[8] was founded in 1925.

It was housed in the Staszic Palace next to the University of Warsaw. Like the school in Paris, it awarded scholarships, and above all attracted a collection of outstanding Polish and French men and women.

Then came the Second World War. The Institute was transferred abroad. A new Francophile diplomatic mission was set up in Kraków in May 1946. This Institut Français was located in the Lubomirski Palace, and the translator and expert in Polish literature Jean Bourilly was named director. Unfortunately, by January 1950, the Institute's activities had been suspended under pressure from the USSR. In 1953 Joseph Stalin died, and in 1958 France introduced a new constitution and became the Fifth Republic. General Charles de Gaulle took power. Bourilly was named cultural attaché to Poland, but soon asked to go on leave. It then occurred to ambassador Étienne Burin des Roziers to turn to his good friend, the young and exceptionally talented Michel Foucault, to replace Bourilly in his post as attaché—though ultimately, Foucault was instead named director of the Cultural Center.

The Center for French Culture was the place of the Warsaw intelligentsia's dreams. Everyone spent time there: from the philosopher Tadeusz Kotarbiński to the novelist Maria

Dąbrowska, from the author Jarosław Iwaszkiewicz to the film director Andrzej Wajda. Antoni Libera wrote in his 1998 novel *Madame* that the moment guests stepped inside, the dizzying aroma of lily-of-the-valley washed over them in a wave, mixed with notes of tobacco. Some remember the smell to this day. People marveled at and delighted in the orange Bic pens, the smell of rubber erasers, the sight of documents sorted into colorful folders. As Foucault was opening the Center, he must have also overseen such basic matters as the interior décor and furnishing the rooms and the library. Yet above all, the Center held a large amount of banned literature, subversive philosophy, and art that socialism's adherents viewed as destructive to human emotions.

The Center quickly became a cult location on the map of Warsaw. And its director, Michel Foucault, became a man of renown.

The Ambassador

The French Embassy in Warsaw was located at 9c Zakopiańska Street.

Étienne Burin des Roziers served as ambassador from September 13, 1958, to January 19, 1962. Throughout this entire period he was surveilled by the secret police. Out of seven volumes of secret files on investigations carried out under the code name "FRANC," one has survived—a few dozen pages and seven pictures.

It says nothing about Foucault.

In a photo from a Foreign Ministry identification form dated August 1958, Burin des Roziers looks like a handsome man dressed in a well-cut suit. He has a high forehead, hair smoothed back, and a handsome smile. He wears a narrow, fashionable tie with a white shirt.

Reports from 1960 describe the ambassador's domestic situation. He was married and had two children, five and seven years old. An aside mentions that during the war, Burin des Roziers's wife was imprisoned in Ravensbrück concentration camp, while he himself served as an artillery officer and Air Force captain.

The agent also listed the new ambassador's personal traits: he was handsome, of medium build, athletic, a hunter. Very direct and easygoing, he knew how to earn friendships and sympathies. He spoke Polish, but poorly. Regarding his political orientation: "naturally a supporter of de Gaulle's policies."

According to the report, the ambassador took his position very seriously and assessed the situation in Poland "realistically." He acknowledged the achievements of the People's Republic, but he didn't overlook the errors and blunders (these included: "excessive bureaucracy, shortcomings in industrial modernization, gaps in planning, poor labor productivity"). Burin des Roziers also described Poland's political position with the Soviet Union "realistically," understanding the country had no other solution.

"Poland is the ground on which the strongest influences of West and East meet," the ambassador said. "And only Poland, as the most significantly liberal state of the socialist bloc, is best suited to establishing enduring relationships between the two camps."

The ambassador was very keen to develop cultural and academic exchanges between Poland and France and—more broadly—between East and West. Yet he ran up against the resistance of Poland's communist authorities. They pointed out inequalities between their two countries in education levels as well as the fact that education in Poland was free, while in the West it cost a fortune. They also feared exchanges of academics and students would lead to information about armaments and nuclear energy leaking out of Poland.

Despite many hours of conversations with Burin des Roziers, the agent stated "there is still no firm indication the Ambassador holds an interest in acquiring any kind of confidential information." What interested Burin des Roziers instead issues like preparing young people for college, birth control initiatives, the position of the Church, French scholarships for Poles, German propaganda, the meager cultivation of Poland's new western territories, as well as rural migration to the cities, poor price planning initiatives, and agricultural policies. The intelligence services concluded these were not particularly interesting topics, much less dangerous ones.

Finally the agent stated: "In conversation, he demonstrated no interests beyond normal ones for a foreigner well acquainted with our internal affairs. He did not demonstrate greater interest in the activities of the Assoc. for the Support of Cultural Cooperation with France, apart from a declaration of aid for any needs we may declare." No needs were declared.

Friendship

Michel Foucault befriended Étienne Burin des Roziers and supported him in every cultural enterprise in Poland.

Burin des Roziers was sent to Poland as one of de Gaulle's closest confidants. He was accompanied by the Compte d'Harcourt, whom one agent—not knowing this was a member of one of the oldest aristocratic families in France—referred to in a memo as "the so-called count" or "former count." D'Harcourt was in charge of holding receptions for prominent figures in culture, the arts, and science. The files note he was sickly, one-legged, and ugly. Moreover, one agent writes: "The Embassy's 1st secretary (Chargé d'Affaires), Mr. d'Harcourt (I believe that is the spelling), was previously stationed in Prague during the war in the Resistance Movement, he fled from the Germans to Spain, despite lacking one leg and being gravely wounded. Very closed-off, taciturn, difficult to form any kind of opinion of him based on a five-minute conversation."

It was probably the Compte d'Harcourt who saw Foucault off, just as a few years later he would see off the departing Ambassador Burin des Roziers (on January 11, 1962). Burin des Roziers was offered either a Polish wolfskin or a silver platter as a parting gift (the choice was left to his wife).

Burin des Roziers remembered Foucault as a cheerful, kind, and youthful academic. "[H]appy to take on a job whose interest, importance, and great difficulty he realized from the start."[9]

Foucault was a caring, open, and energetic person with a sunny disposition. He didn't talk down to his friends and colleagues, instead appearing approachable and interested. He was a people person.

Burin des Roziers wrote that Foucault "[put] in an appearance at cultural events in the four corners of Poland, observing with a certain amount of indulgence and amusement the somewhat vain rites of diplomatic mumbo jumbo."[10] Yet his curiosity about hermetic societies, exclusion, and the socialist system caused him trouble. His Polish friends warned him this might happen. Defert recalls Michel could have expected problems—the police and intelligence services were interested in him.

And he was gay, after all.

At Every Step

Late in the fall of 1958, Burin des Roziers traveled north, to the Baltic coast. He and the group of people accompanying him stayed at the Grand Hotel in Sopot, and the next day headed to the town of Puck to go fishing.

It's very possible Foucault went along with the ambassador. His friend might have wanted to show him the beauty of this country where he intended to live. At the time, Puck was still a fishing settlement, not popular with tourists. Small fishing boats were moored at the harbor and trees covered the hills. The beach was completely empty—half of it was scattered with enormous nets hanging on wooden stakes to dry in the wind and sunlight.

The ambassador and his party were checked into rooms that had been "technically secured." The secret police also considered it essential to establish which buildings the ambassador would want to visit (so agents could be sent in) as well as which Polish citizens would attend the reception held in his honor.

These activities obviously had to be carried out discreetly, with all the results and materials sent without delay to the appropriate department of the Ministry of Internal Affairs.

Though the report contains a description of the security and bugging devices, all the names of Ambassador Burin des Roziers's companions are missing.

New Year's Eve 1962

The last report in Burin des Roziers's file comes from January 1962. The ambassador had finished his service in Poland. Two official farewells took place.

In his speech at the first reception, at the embassy, Burin des Roziers declared in ungrammatical Polish that he could never forget this country.

The second farewell took place on Senatorska Street in the Ministry of Culture and Art.

"Apparently there were over six hundred people present, drawn from representatives of the authorities and Polish society," reported an agent. "Once the ambassador departs, his duties will be taken over by d'Harcourt, who as Chargé d'Affaires will carry out his duties for an extended period. As yet there is no information about who has been named the new Ambassador, meanwhile Burin des Roziers is apparently to take up a post in Vienna."

Burin des Roziers made a positive impression on the intelligence services. It appears he was unimpeachable. So it was noted that "he is despotic in relation to his closest associates, and his relationship with his wife, though proper, has not prevented him from having various dalliances." Such "dalliances" make frequent appearances in the files of people the services had difficulty pinning more serious lapses on. A person's private life was always the easiest thing to exploit.

Evidently the ambassador's greatest passion during his time in Poland was hunting. So perhaps the farewell gift his wife chose was the wolfskin, rather than the silver platter.

Arnaud

Burin des Roziers's successor was Pierre Charpentier. Michel Foucault's replacement as director of the Center for French Culture was Pierre Arnaud (codename: "Prudent").

Arnaud arrived in Warsaw on October 17, 1959. Unfortunately, we don't know if Foucault did an official handover at the Center. He had probably already left Warsaw. Arnaud moved into Foucault's old apartment at 32 Rutkowski Street.

The surveillance machine sprang into action.

Opening a file on Arnaud was justified by "the need to monitor an employee of a capitalist university mission in Poland," so the report on Michel Foucault might have said something similar. The secret police memo declared that Pierre Arnaud had been on the staff of the General Directorate for Cultural and Technical Affairs in the French foreign ministry since 1958, and previously had been posted to Dublin and New York. In 1959, he received an independent post in the Principality of Monaco, and then, at his own request, was transferred to Warsaw to become the Director of the Center for French Culture at the University of Warsaw.

The report notes with dismay that "the materials we possess show P. Arnaud in his activities as director of the Center for French Culture has long since transgressed the limits permitted by the international agreement."

What did that mean?

Although the Center operated at the University of Warsaw and was therefore in the capital, Arnaud's activities covered the whole country. Additionally, and by agreement with the French Embassy, he was one of the unofficial leaders behind the activities of the Polish Association for the Support of Academic Collaboration with France, whose local centers gathered academic staff from practically every college and university in Poland, for the benefit of French policy. Arnaud was professionally engaged and actually performed his duties, which the agents regarded as unusual and suspicious.

Despite reservations and doubts regarding Arnaud, in the end his work was well received. He left Poland on April 1, 1961. The file on codename "Prudent" was closed.

But one detail is particularly interesting.

Arnaud, according to one of the agents, "during his time here maintained a string of intimate relationships with Polish women." We don't know if this was true. But it made it into the files.

The differences between the first and second directors of the Center for French Culture in Poland are twofold.

Firstly, files exist documenting the surveillance of Arnaud; there are no such files on Foucault.

Secondly, despite the information on both men's intimate relationships, only Foucault was forced to leave the country because of them. This means the issue was not having intimate relationships with Polish citizens in general, but the government's attitude toward homosexuality in particular. We could say it was not Foucault's own homosexuality per se that drove the philosopher out of Poland, just as Arnaud's "intimate contacts" with Polish women were not a reason to cut his tenure short. Instead, it was the authorities' own homophobia that sealed Foucault's fate.

But can we be sure?

Cocteau

In October 1960, the *Quinzaine Française* festival of French culture took place in Warsaw, Wrocław, and Kraków. It was a packed program: conferences, film screenings, artistic exhibitions, debates.

One featured guest was the writer, director, and painter Jean Cocteau. He was received with great pomp. He stayed and ate at the Bristol, toured Warsaw, paid a visit to the Iwaszkiewiczes at their country villa, and met many people from the worlds of politics and culture. He conversed with important writers and artists such as Jan Parandowski, Antoni Słonimski, Franciszek Starowieyski, and Alina Szapocznikow.

The papers wrote about him. *Życie Warszawy* recommended Cocteau's latest movie, *Testament of Orpheus*.[11]

Jean Cocteau was thrilled.

The festival preparations were certainly labor- and time-intensive. It was Foucault who had borne the brunt of the organization.

Yet he himself was not invited.

Exactly one year earlier, Foucault had left Warsaw, under a cloud of infamy.

Extradition

Since homosexuality was not a criminal offense in Poland, the government needed to find an excuse to extradite Foucault.

Accusations of paying for sex would be the easiest way. That being said, if the allegations against Arnaud were true, finding appropriate women would have been much easier. Getting rid of Foucault was potentially more difficult not only because homosexuality was legal, but because he didn't use male prostitutes. In this situation the only option was to find, coerce, and introduce him to a suitable individual.

If Foucault was being surveilled just like Arnaud and if material was being collected on him, this sort of information-gathering must have been taking place on many levels.

For instance, "operational activities (PP, PDF) were conducted" on one French lecturer in Kraków named Christian J., "as a result of which the sexual perversion of the aforementioned was established." Despite this, there is no information that the lecturer—a gay man whose "delinquency" had been proven—was made to abandon Poland.

PP stood for *podsłuch pokojowy*—room surveillance, and PDF was *podgląd dokumentowany filmowo lub fotograficznie*—surveillance documented by film or photography. The same methods were certainly used on Foucault. The material gathered, was, in both cases, likely destroyed.

Arnaud had intimate relations with Polish women.

Christian J. met up with boys in Kraków without getting in trouble.

Cocteau—who was gay—was fêted in Poland.

So the question is: why was Michel Foucault in particular such a problem for the Polish People's Republic?

Goodbye, See You Tomorrow

Françoise Bourbon[12] was fifteen when she met Michel Foucault. Her father was the consul in Gdańsk, where the philosopher had come along with a group of young people for a conference on recent French literature.

"He was wonderful, full of life, a charming man," says Françoise today. "My father and Ambassador Burin des Roziers were equally delighted with him. He was very intelligent, as well as cheerful and easy to talk to."

Foucault spent a few days in Gdańsk in the summer of 1959. People in the French community talked about how every foreigner had someone tailing them. Everyone, including Foucault, knew they were constantly being watched. But the French loved Poland and the Poles.

"It was a strange mix of fear and delight," Françoise Bourbon emphasizes. "Even with our awareness of the [post-Stalinist] Thaw it wasn't easy, but Foucault, who was interested in forms of bondage, maybe had even more of an uphill battle."

Bondage might be associated with the communist political system.

"Maybe," wonders Madame Bourbon, "that was the very reason he was removed from Poland."

Bourbon recalls Michel Foucault always left their home laden with packages and food that her mother had prepared. He would catch the train for Warsaw carrying many days' worth of provisions. He never refused.

Someone as interested as Foucault was in prisons, regimentation, violence, and repression could not be allowed to sleep soundly in a country in the grip of communist madness. So the authorities needed to find an excuse for deportation, formulate a plan, and throw Foucault out of Poland.

History of Madness

Michel Foucault's doctoral dissertation, which he wrote in large measure in Warsaw, was published in France in 1961 under the title *Folie et déraison. L'histoire de la folie à l'âge classique.* This book was not published in Poland until 1987.

In the preface to the first French edition—not included in the Polish edition—Foucault wrote that work on his dissertation began "in the course of a Swedish night" and was "finished in the stubborn, bright sun of Polish liberty."[13]

Foucault wrote to a friend in a letter from Warsaw, "You know that *Ubu* takes place in Poland, meaning nowhere. I am in prison [. . .]. Clouds rise ceaselessly off the Vistula. We have forgotten what light is. They have put me up in a socialist palace. I am working on my *Madness*, which, in this whirl of delirium, risks becoming a bit too much of what it was always meant to be."[14]

Ubu Roi is a play by the turn-of-the-century genius and madman Alfred Jarry. The action takes place in Poland, which is ruled by the cruel and grotesque Ubu after a coup against King Wenceslas. Once the rightful heir to the throne, Prince Boggerlas, seizes back power, Ubu flees to France.

Foucault stayed briefly at the Hotel Bristol, after which he transferred to a private apartment. There is no evidence that he rented the apartment personally; it was probably arranged by the Embassy, since Foucault's successor, Pierre Arnaud, also lived on Rutkowski Street. But maybe Michel found the apartment himself, and once he was gone the Embassy took it over, so to speak. We can be sure that whenever he traveled outside of Warsaw, whether to see the rest of the country or fly to Paris, he would leave the keys to the apartment with Stefan or Jurek. He was indifferent to material things.

It must not have been easy for Foucault to write his dissertation without access to publications and sources, outside the realm of the French language. Perhaps he drew inspiration from the madness surrounding him.

An example: according to Defert, Miss Borowska—Foucault's secretary in Warsaw—wanted very much to impress him, and so she moved heaven and earth to acquire two lemons. She offered the Frenchman this most fabulous of presents, washed and wrapped in paper. Foucault accepted the lemons, peeled them, squeezed the juice into a glass, and downed it in a single gulp. Miss Borowska was speechless, she couldn't believe her eyes. Such expensive lemons, in a single gulp? Only years later did Foucault understand the significance of that incident, when Miss Borowska visited him in Paris and told him about the shock he'd given her with his offhand attitude toward the lemons.

Without a doubt, *History of Madness* was Foucault's attempt to understand himself, his otherness, which was simultaneously his true identity. It was also the gateway to his research on sexuality. Madness, after all, was a category of social exclusion in the same way as homosexuality. You need only switch the two words around.

In the book that he wrote in Warsaw, Foucault was talking about himself.

On Christmas 1958, he submitted the first draft of his dissertation to his supervisor. In response he received one sentence: "Don't change a thing, this is a doctorate."[15]

Before All This Happened

Paul-Michel Foucault was born on October 15, 1926, in Poitiers into a family of the bourgeois intelligentsia. His father, Paul-André Foucault, was a doctor and his mother, Anne-Marie Malapert, was the daughter of a surgeon. As a woman, she herself was unable to study medicine. Paul-Michel had a sister one year older and a brother seven years younger, who also became a surgeon. When he was older, Paul-Michel very quickly went against his father's wishes and declared he would never follow in his footsteps.

He spent the war with his family on his maternal grandmother's estate.

In 1945, after graduating from high school, he enrolled in a two-year preparatory program to study at the prestigious École Normale Supérieure in Paris. This was an especially difficult period for him. He felt different among his college friends.

He attempted suicide several times.

He ended up in psychoanalysis.

In 1950 he joined the Communist Party.

The musician Gilbert Humbert, a friend of Foucault's during this period, wrote in his memoirs that in those days, Michel was very quiet and shy. He could recite the poems of Musset and Nerval from memory. He read Husserl and Jaspers. He was attracted to Bergson's "liminal experiences." He was fascinated with death and suffering.

"Foucault was intelligent like all homosexuals," recalled Maurice Pinguet, a friend from college.

Starting in 1951, Foucault couldn't get his mind off quitting the Communist Party and going far away from France for a long time.

In May 1952 he started a relationship with the composer Jean Barraqué.

At the age of twenty-six, Foucault was obsessed with surrealism, listening to Beethoven, reading Nietzsche and Kafka. He saw *Waiting for Godot* in the theater, a moment he considered a turning point in his life.

He wanted to break up with his partner.

In October of that year he resigned his party membership.

He couldn't wait to leave France.

He was drinking heavily. He had depressive episodes.

In 1956, he moved to Uppsala.

He threw himself into his dissertation.

The History of Reason

History of Madness is a dispute between reason and unreason, the desire to gain knowledge of that which falls outside of knowledge, which itself is anti-knowledge, the conflict of reason and madness. Foucault asks: how do we know madness is madness? How do we define what is mad? How can reason grasp unreason?

Another potential question: How can a nonhomosexual understand a homosexual?

There can be no knowledge of that which falls outside of knowledge. Madness is the lack of knowledge. That is why Foucault's dissertation does not address the history of these concepts (because they did not exist), but rather the archeology of silence (that whereof one cannot speak).

Madness and homosexuality are similar to one another. As long as there is no knowledge about them—medical, statistical, political—they do not exist. Or rather: they are left in peace. When knowledge emerges, so too does a sense of danger. To gain knowledge of a thing means putting it under the microscope.

The worst thing for outsiders is ignorance, which causes fear. Moreover, knowledge always only touches on some concept of an object, not the entirety of the fact. As the secret police agents gathered material on gay people, they were seeking a pathology that would give them the certainty that they had everything under control. In his dissertation, Foucault described this same mechanism in relation to madness.

What better place for Michel Foucault to write his dissertation than socialist Poland?

Freedom Cannot Exist Without Enslavement

If Foucault had set out to investigate conspicuous silences, what he achieved was describing the mechanisms of rejection. Writing became a process of recovering our conceptions of freedom, because reason could not exist without madness, heterosexuality without homosexuality, femininity without masculinity, good without evil, or freedom without enslavement.

Michel Foucault saw his experience in Warsaw as a conflict between desires and reality. But because he was a man of the West, not a socialist man enslaved to imagination, this alienation became a process of internal transformation.

He felt safe.

Nothing could threaten him.

Even a trap laid by the secret police could only fascinate him, not truly frighten him.

On the one hand he had a Westerner's special freedom, protected by international treaties, the Embassy's privileges, the presumption that global conflict could ensue from his actual enslavement.

On the other hand he knew that one day he would leave Warsaw and go home.

Can we seriously investigate our own identity while a secret agent sits at the next table, noting down our every gesture?

Can we truly fear our sexuality being exposed in a world where sex takes place in public bathrooms?

Can we limit our fantasies when we can make them come completely true for as little as the cost of a bottle of vodka?

Perhaps in enslaved Warsaw, Foucault was—for the only time in his life—truly free. This is why he called the cold sun, darkened by autumn fog rolling off the Vistula, "the stubborn sun of freedom."

Where everything is madness, anything is possible.

Illusion

Knowledge about madness is the illusion of knowledge about anything. Such an illusion, such knowledge about the lack of knowledge, can provoke feelings of anxiety and dismay. Yet it can also make us aware of our freedom. Foucault says: now there's nothing I cannot do, nothing I should do, I can do anything.

Was Foucault lonely in Warsaw?

Did he feel trapped?

Could he be happy, even sometimes?

In the preface to his book he mentions his gratitude to three people—Georges Dumézil, Jean Hyppolite, and Georges Canguilhem.

No one Polish.

And yet. The closing paragraph of the preface to *History of Madness* reads: "I should also name many others who appear not to matter. Yet they know, these friends from Sweden and these Polish friends, that there is something of their presence in these pages. May they pardon me for making such demands on them and their happiness, they who were so close to a work that spoke only of distant sufferings, and the slightly dusty archives of pain."[16]

"Distant sufferings" and "archives of pain."

Is that what Poland was to Foucault?

What could these words mean within the dual otherness and feelings of exclusion Foucault must have been experiencing? He was spending time with friends and young men, but he was a stranger. With every step, at every moment of the day and night. Now that he had all that behind him, he saw this as a long-ago suffering, an experience of pain with the potential to bear fruit as a dissertation on madness.

Ship of Fools

Exclusion creates spaces in which the excluded are not excluded from one another.

Stultifera navis ("ship of fools") is the first chapter of Foucault's book.

This was based on real events. Madmen were put on ships and sent out to sea. The people still on land felt safe. They felt no guilt, they did not believe they had acted immorally.

A few hundred years later trains left the Umschlagplatz, carrying people to the gas chambers. Those who perpetrated this were convinced they were acting rightly. They thought they were defending their identity against the disease of otherness.

Foucault must have seen the place in Warsaw from which the Jews were deported to Treblinka. He also surely knew where the boundaries of the ghetto had been. He must have realized that in writing about the exclusion of madness, he was writing about the madness of exclusion.

Lepers, the insane, the ill, unbelievers, Jews, Gypsies, refugees from Syria, homosexuals—all excluded from the spaces of "normal" people, of Michel Foucault himself, who was recording their story within a world of political alienation.

Foucault understood that exclusion always turns against the excluders. Maybe this was yet another reason he felt no fear in Poland, away from freedom. After all, he knew that in the history of the world, evil had never yet won out. He also knew that coming of age is an extended process, and pupation has to happen slowly. Socialist Warsaw likely fascinated him because he perceived it as a city of future liberation.

The insane political system he was experiencing firsthand was evidence of one of his main theses: that madness occurs only in a society of normal people.

Madness was invented, like race, like society, and like sexuality.

Departure

In 1959, a UFO crashed near Gdynia, meat sales were suspended on Mondays, Nixon came to Poland, Fidel Castro seized power in Cuba, an apparition of the Virgin Mary appeared in Warsaw's Nowolipki, Jaroslaw Iwaszkiewicz became chairman of the Polish Writers' Union, and the world laid eyes on the Barbie doll for the first time.

At the end of May, an exhibition of French paintings (from Gauguin to the abstract artists) opened at the National Museum in Warsaw. Michel Foucault must have seen it and was perhaps taken less with the paintings than with the copious ceramic vases standing in the exhibition halls, overflowing with poppies and other wildflowers. They were so impressive that the press even covered them.

Although Foucault had plans for his time Poland—he wanted to build up Francophile and cultural activity, personally oversee recruitment of Slavists to positions at various institutions, cultivate the network of Instituts Français in Warsaw, Kraków, and other cities—he had to leave Warsaw.

"A clear, precise, and penetrating intellect with a wealth of great culture," wrote Jean Bourilly in an opinion of him, "Michel Foucault possesses a sense of authority. He is capable of fulfilling important foreign functions most satisfactorily, whether in a teaching position or in a position that includes administrative responsibilities. In his direction of the Centre d'Études at the university, a post he took on from 1958 to 1959, he had to confront numerous difficulties, which involved material conditions (the absence of any location for the center, or an apartment for himself, for many months) as much as they involved the specific nature and aims of the center itself. He was, nonetheless, able to guarantee a propitious beginning for this new Franco-Polish organization."[17]

Not a word on the true problems, the actual reasons for his departure, or the atmosphere in which Foucault spent his year in Warsaw.

The summer vacation passed. Foucault left Warsaw for Paris, then Hamburg, where he lectured for a few months on French theater, but where he primarily ran the local Institut Français, and in the company of Roland Barthes, Alain Robbe-Grillet, and Jean Bruce often visited the nightlife district of St. Pauli. In some strip clubs and bars, the customers and staff knew him as *"Herr Doktor."* This is where he discovered transvestism, thanks to which he soon wrote his momentous piece on Herculine Barbin.[18]

The time of Foucault's voluntary exile was coming to an end. After five years, he returned home.

Solidarity 1982

Martial law was declared in Poland on December 13, 1981.

A day later, French Minister of Foreign Affairs Claude Cheysson declared that France would not intervene in Poland's internal affairs. Michel Foucault and Pierre Bourdieu protested. They asserted the French government's inaction was immoral and mendacious. Foucault's letter of protest was published in *Libération* on December 15, 1982: "The French government must not, like Moscow and Washington, make us believe that setting up a military dictatorship in Poland is an internal affair, leaving the Polish people with the ability to choose their own fate. This is an untrue and immoral assertion . . . In 1936, a socialist government found itself confronted with a military putsch in Spain; in 1956, a socialist government found itself confronted with repression in Hungary. In 1981, a socialist government is confronted with the coup in Warsaw. We do not want it to take the same attitude as its predecessors. We remind [the government] of its promise to assert the obligations of international moral standards against the obligations of Realpolitik."[19]

Popular support for the Solidarity movement in France was enormous. At first, *Libération* tried to print a list of the petition's signatories, but they swiftly reconsidered—there were simply too many. The letter led directly to a fifty-thousand-person demonstration taking to the streets of Paris, supporting Foucault and protesting the situation in Poland.

Foucault and Bourdieu's petition—also signed by Marguerite Duras, Patrice Chéreau, Simone Signoret, and Yves Montand—was met with negative reactions from some, including *Le Monde* director Jacques Fauvet, Secretary of the Socialist Party Lionel Jospin, and Minister of Culture Jack Lang. Meanwhile, the French Democratic Confederation of Labor supported the Solidarity trade union and formed a support committee for the Poles.

On September 22, 1982, Michel Foucault set off for Poland along with Simone Signoret, Dr. Bernard Kouchner, Jacques Lebas, and Jean-Pierre Mauber from the organization Médecins du Monde. They were bringing humanitarian aid: their truck was full of medicine and banned publications.

We know from Kouchner's recollections that the whole journey took place in a fairly relaxed and cheerful atmosphere. For fun, Foucault and Signoret acted out characters from the Tintin comics, told jokes, sang songs from the repertoires of Edith Piaf and Montand, and shared stories from their lives. Foucault told his friends about his first stay in Warsaw.

This time everyone stayed at the Victoria Hotel, which had a view of the Tomb of the Unknown Soldier. They were received by the minister of health, who thanked them for their gifts. Foucault refused to shake his hand.[20]

After returning to France, Foucault and Signoret reported on their trip on television. The actress wore a Solidarity symbol pinned to her jacket lapel.

This operation on Poland's behalf was the last manifestation of Michel Foucault's political activity. The journey to Warsaw sent him on the trail of his own past, to a city where he had lived, worked, and loved. He returned to honor what he had described in the preface to *History of Madness* as the stubborn sun of Polish liberty.

Before his trip to Warsaw he wrote his will.

Two years later, on June 25, 1984, at 1:15 P.M., Michel Foucault died in Paris, of AIDS.

Once All This Has Passed

Michel Foucault died in Paris's Salpêtrière Hospital, which he had described in *History of Madness*. The philosopher was transferred to a building where, a century earlier, Sigmund Freud's mentor, Dr. Jean-Martin Charcot, had conducted research on hypnosis and hysteria.

History had come full circle.

"Foucault knew perfectly well he was suffering from AIDS," says Daniel Defert. "Of course, he was still writing, he was editing articles and planning new ones. Of course, he also had plans to travel to Andalusia. But he knew."

Foucault had hoped that he was someone whom the "American disease"—"gay cancer," "the sodomites' punishment"— had bypassed. That his symptoms were in reality something entirely trivial.

But they were not.

Was he afraid to die?

He knew there was no treatment, that his time was passing quickly, that nothing and no one could save him. He was not a natural malcontent. The depressive episodes of his youth that drove him to attempt suicide were certainly not the result of momentary drops in mood or desire for attention.

Foucault was serious.

He therefore took his illness seriously, and perhaps this was what liberated him from the panicked response that is so common in unavoidable situations.

Michel Foucault was not afraid to die.

Maybe instead he was curious about the end—at least as a philosopher.

On the day Michel Foucault died, the offices of the most important French newspapers and magazines received a short wire: "Michel Foucault is dead." And all hell broke loose—a hell made up of information, gossip about Foucault's life, and who had authority over his body.

As usual, Daniel Defert remained somewhat in the shadows. Yet this was the first moment in which the shadows became interesting. From them on, he would always have to answer questions about Foucault.

When *Le Monde* wrote about Foucualt's death, it suggested he had died of a nerve disease. But a small note at the bottom of the page in left-wing *Libération* caused an explosion of scandal. The author said the suggestion Foucault had been killed by AIDS was "virulent" slander that implied Foucault had "died in shame."[21] The uproar caused by this disgraceful article opened a new chapter in the public discussion of AIDS and increased awareness of the disease itself.

"Foucault's work seems to me the most important event of thought in our century,"[22] wrote historian and close friend of Foucault, Paul Veyne, a few days later. Condolences were coming in from everywhere, everyone had something to say about the philosopher and his passing.

People spoke of national mourning and France losing a gem, that the world had bid farewell to the most outstanding mind of our times, that there would never be such an intellectual again.

The only person who remained silent was Daniel Defert.

In attendance at a ceremony in front of the Parisian hospital building on June 29 were: Simone Signoret, Yves Montand, Paul Veyne, Pierre Bourdieu, Georges Canguilhem, Bernard Kouchner, Claude Mauriac, and many others. The philosopher Gilles Deleuze gave a speech. He read an excerpt of the most recent part of Michel Foucault's final work, *The History of Sexuality*.

The coffin of blond wood was placed on two small and unstable-looking trusses. TV cameras were recording everything, and pictures were taken by a young photographer who leaned against the wall.

Foucault was interred that same day in Vendeuvre-du-Poitou, where he liked to spend his summer vacations and where the ashes of his family lay. Only his family and closest friends were present at the burial.

His tombstone reads: "Paul-Michel Foucault, Professeur du Collège de France, 1926–1984."

After the ceremony, Michel Foucault's mother, Anne-Marie Malapert, went up to Daniel Defert and told him:

"You were just his friend. You will write nothing about him."

And so it was.

Will

Just before his final trip to Poland in September 1982, Michel Foucault wrote his will. It was three sentences long, two of which are known:

"Death, not invalidism."

"No posthumous publications."

The point was that if Michel Foucault lost consciousness, he would not be kept alive artificially. Nor did he want his books, texts, works—even those already finished or with the editors—to come out after his death.

Daniel Defert claims that Foucault was in a dispute with the author Marguerite Yourcenar about the relationship between a writer, their texts, and their audience. Yourcenar believed a text comes alive after its author's death. Foucault said it died with its creator.

The fourth part of *The History of Sexuality* is currently being prepared for printing.

The part that was never meant to be published.

"It's not particularly interesting," admits Daniel Defert, "but in the end, it's Foucault."

At the edges of the community, at town gates,
large, barren, uninhabitable areas appeared,
where the disease no longer reigned but its ghost still hovered.
For centuries, these spaces would belong to the domain of the inhuman.

History of Madness

ON THE TRAIL

Madame Janusz's Story

"It wasn't particularly hard to meet a soldier," Janusz tells me. "For instance, on the corner of Świętokrzyska and Emilia Plater, there's this little rotunda, where forty boys at a time from the military Honor Guards would go on leave on Sundays. They'd come for a beer and us girls would try to pick them up. One hundred percent success rate. You can take my word for it, I know precisely how it worked.

"A girlfriend of mine, who was taken from us on account of being a drunk, was named Zbyszek. She had a stall at the stadium market, business was good, she liked a good time. She used to have those soldiers by the barrelful. Not necessarily for money, or not always, anyway, and not with just anybody. But they didn't think twice about it, absolutely not. In any case, there were a few different forms it could take. If a fellow was expecting to cruise aimlessly around the city with his friends, he might prefer being taken to a private party. It also depended who was asking, anyway, and how they were asking. I knew a soldier who came to see me right until his service was over and he didn't hold back one bit.

"The soldiers got their fair share out of it. They'd get a couple złotys, drink up, eat, and have a night of passion to boot. Getting a hard-on is nothing for a young buck like that, even the touch of a little butterfly will set him off. We've got some fellows like that nowadays too—bisexuals! But the days of the soldiers are long gone. The gay clubs came in, so now a girlfriend goes to one of these places where there's a few hundred boys—why pick up a soldier, and then on top of everything else, have to explain how it all works? What for? It's different nowadays, we've got much more awareness of the community now. It used to be you'd cruise slowly, methodically. I'd meet one of these boys, say, three times. He'd eat and drink for free, but I wouldn't whisper a word about sex, only about girls, to stop him from catching on. And if something happened, it would only be at the very end of the night.

"Even so, you had to watch your back. There were some girlfriends who got beaten up too, and even killed, like that colonel, that was a notorious case. I was very careful. I take everything in visually; if I liked someone, then I'd get the pleasure of passing time with him, even the pleasure of spending money on him, the pleasure of an embrace. These days I'm left with nothing but these sort of father-son instincts. Sex doesn't interest me anymore.

"There's one I remember in particular. He was one hundred percent male. At the moment he's retired, a colonel, and in the army he was a unit commander. We're in touch to this day. He's got a wife and two kids. He got married because he'd had a slipup or two and otherwise they'd have chucked him out of the army. I met him at the beer stand actually, by that rotunda. And he was such a little hooligan, such a rascal. Once we were walking along, one of our girls came up to him and gives him a little, how's it going, sweetie? And my friend gave this queen such a smack in the mouth that he drew blood and he said: I might be a fucking sweetie, but not for you. It just goes to show that you had to win someone over in order to have him and experience him later on.

"To pick up a straight boy took patience and maybe a sense of humor. My mother was an actress, I think I inherited her ability to, if you like, sort of behave in different ways. And besides I worked in television, spent time around people, so it somehow got into my blood. Apart from the soldiers there were also the roughnecks, as we called them: these crafty little buggers with with gummy ears, crusty noses, and a grin like a train track. And one of these comes up to me once and asks: hey buddy, you got a smoke? I say: for you? Of course. I take out a cigarette and I give it to him. And now it's a whole different ball game. I've caught him by surprise. So I keep up the momentum and say: all right, take an extra one for yourself. And now I'm a friend.

"That's how I used to win men over, and afterward my girlfriends would say: you're not scared of them one bit, they warm up to you and then you're all best pals. And I said: I just know how to adapt. I got it from my mother, the actress."

Different Methods of Cruising

Queer life existed on a sort of trail: the mushroom on Three Crosses Square, another one on Zieleniecka, and a third on Dąbrowski.

"But they wiped all that out, capitalism came and it was over."

"It's a story that's impossible to tell, because it was like a peacock of paradise."

"Or a unicorn!"

"Or both."

And my two contacts tell the story.

"Once I picked up this handsome guy on the street. I said something and he said something back, and now we're walking along together and talking. I open with: you're such an outgoing, great guy, I'd love to take you out for a coffee. But he was sharp and goes: man, aren't you wasting your time on me, aren't you better off picking up some girl? And that opened my eyes, that if somebody's on the ball and not interested, he'll say no. I've also got this personal theory that every good-looking guy in Warsaw must have had a brush with gayness, because there were so many gays out cruising in all kinds of situations that the only way to avoid it was by being ugly."

"You'd get lots of different situations with cruising. One girlfriend did it where she pretended to be a TV director. My, she had a lot of nerve! She'd go to the beer stand on Świętokrzyska and promise the boys a career in television. Which put her in very high demand."

"There was one rule: never mess around with vodka! All my friends who died, it was because they drank too much. It was really dangerous if you were into trade. Because you had to stay on the ball, you never knew for sure why he kept meeting up with you."

"There were different methods of cruising. There was no buying sight unseen, you'd know what someone looked like from the get-go, which was an advantage. That's why everyone liked hitting up the cruising spots. There were tons of urinals. And so the queers would do a circuit of the mushrooms, moving from one to the other. The metal barrier was high enough off the ground that you could count the legs. The police would drive up and if they saw legs grouped together, they'd storm in from both ends and go hunting. They'd arrest one guy and the rest would skedaddle."

"Once on Zieleniecka it was just me and another guy. I leaned over a little toward him and he toward me, and he goes, it's dangerous here, let's head out. You could never trust somebody a hundred percent, but I figured he was doing me a favor, since I was doing him one, which was normal—but also, he was, you know, this hot, butch boy, it was worth going. So we head out. Further along there's a meadow, he goes come on, we'll settle in down there. And then out of nowhere he stops and suddenly goes: you son of a bitch, and he's got me by the throat. Another three of them jump up out of the blue. I'm not such a useless old piece of shit and so I gave him one right in the jaw. Apparently I hit him good, I tore free and started running, but they surrounded me like hyenas, four against one. I remember like it was yesterday, one of them was this brawny ox, gorgeous! They threw themselves on me. I thought maybe I was getting robbed. I had a gold watch, so I somehow ripped off the watch and, as I'm defending myself, slipped it into my pants. One was choking me and pulling my hair, he whacked me at the base of my skull and knocked me out. I don't know what happened, apparently someone started hollering because then they ran away and I got out of the whole thing unscathed."

"That's what our gay era was like. A terrible way to live— first of all, the police chasing after you, pummeling you with truncheons, you'd run away, then get dragged into headquarters for interrogation; and second of all, there was no normal way of meeting people, and murders were the order of the day."

"I found it all incredibly exciting because, come on, these were hardly everyday experiences."

Lulla

Lulla says the life of a queen isn't all foundation and blush.

Her other comment is that there are two things she can't believe: that there are no files on her and that she didn't know Foucault personally.

The rest comes as no surprise.

She lives in Targówek district, by the Rampa Theater. She likes going there, to see Krystyna Janda perform, for instance. Lulla's an actress herself. She knows Gabriela Zapolska's classic *The Morality of Mrs. Dulska* like the back of her hand, and performed in it in two apartment performances during Martial Law, both to great acclaim.

Lulla has a slim figure, gray hair, and a cheerful disposition.

Lulla does not have a steady husband, the pension she deserves, or a large apartment.

The walls of her studio apartment are painted salmon.

On one is a picture of Marilyn Monroe, on another, a plasma screen. In the corner—a small table, and on it stand framed photos: grandparents, parents, lovers, and Lulla in a red sequined dress, a boa, and a brimmed hat, like a movie star.

Lulla speaks colorfully and precisely. But she's kept silent since morning. She's like an opera singer: first she has to loosen up her throat, stretch her vocal cords, well, just start living. She's not in the habit of talking to the walls; if someone phones too early, at the wrong time, she can be standoffish. By evening she's more gregarious. She starts from the beginning:

"I was born in Warsaw in August of '33, to my father Stefan. Let me tell you about the people I've known ever since I fell, you might say, into this life. As concerns Foucault, I know he was a man who attracted a circle of mainly students, young lads, the flower of Warsaw. From the stories I've heard—you see, I was never at his home—the atmosphere was always elegant, with excellent drinks. He had money, he was from the outside world, and that meant happiness was waiting around every corner for him in Warsaw. But since people are the way they are, it was over before it really began. And that, darling, is life.

"In those days we didn't have our own apartments, everyone either lived with family or rented a little room at someone else's place. Back then it wasn't popular to rent an entire apartment, because people didn't have the means to live separately, or to have a second place to rent out. So everybody lived with their parents instead, and it was only afterward you'd get a place, through work, after college. Then housing cooperatives came along and you could get a foothold. I paid into one myself. For all the money I put up I ought to have gotten a bigger space, but I've got what I've got. They had a rule that as a single person I wasn't eligible for more. Well anyway, what use would I have for a giant apartment, sitting here all by my lonesome?"

There are snacks on the table at Lulla's: tiny herrings, tiny pickles, tiny cocktail tomatoes with feta, chicory with little pieces of cheese and anchovy. Vodka by the glass, orange juice, or tonic water to sip. Toasts are raised and shots are downed. Lightweights may drink half. Latecomers get penalty drinks.

Lulla gets out her albums and shows me her photos. Many are of gorgeous young men, parties, crazy drag queens, well-known personalities. A few are of soldiers.

Soldiers from the Tomb

Lulla never found uniforms particularly attractive.

"But for some of us in the family, uniforms were their sole obsession. They'd go straight to those boys from the Honor Guard in front of the Tomb of the Unknown Soldier and try to score. They'd drive up in their cars and motorcycles and kick up a fuss, and this poor soldier boy, who couldn't breathe a word, what was he supposed to do? He just kept standing there. Which on the one hand made things easier, but on the other was an obstacle. Because how could he get a date when he's stuck there like a post not making a peep, just staring at you from under his cap. You could never be sure that stare meant 'yes' or 'no.' But you'd try anyway, because it was such a hoot.

"There was an army unit at the corner of Szwedzka Street and Solidarność Avenue. For a while the soldiers would get leave once a week and they'd take their leave in their uniforms. I'm told that the area around Stalowa, Szwedzka, and Solidarność was sometimes heaving with our fellow queens with a fetish for uniforms. They'd invite soldiers to dinner, a beer, a cocktail, and then hop in a car and hit the road to jump in the sack.

"Since it was the People's Republic and there were no other options, that Foucault of yours would have been all over it. The Bristol's hardly a stone's throw from the Tomb. Add him rolling up in his Jaguar or even in a taxi or a chauffeured embassy limo, I mean, who could say no to that? Seducing the soldier boys got shut down in the '80s by the government's press secretary, who thought it beggared belief that Western tourists were corrupting our socialist Polish military in exchange for dollars. Though they used to go for złotys and rubles, too.

"Past the Tomb is the Saxon Garden. Being the first public park in Poland, on the gay scene it was always a famously popular cruising spot. Guards on break from the Tomb would hang out on the benches and they'd drink whatever you brought them, and then you'd make plans for a rendezvous. You could also sneak straight up to the Tomb and anonymously slip a bit of paper with your address or a time and place for a tryst into the pockets of their army jackets. That always worked."

Fortunes and Palaces Gone

The most important supplies to have were vodka and kiełbasa.

No soldier could resist them. People lost fortunes, because buying a case of vodka and five kilos of kiełbasa every day was by no means easy. The absolute wealthiest sold off greenhouses, apartments, and all their foreign currency to host soldiers.

Somewhere in Warsaw there's at least one photo album with five hundred pictures of Honor Guards. Indescribable.

How many liters of vodka and kilos of kiełbasa did it take to get five hundred soldiers?

Scandals and Misunderstandings

On several occasions, this passion for Honor Guard men exploded into scandal and misunderstanding. The police had no idea that ladies weren't the only ones who loved a man in uniform, so when certain men kept meeting up with the soldiers it was occasionally interpreted as attempted counterintelligence.

As far back as the early 1950s, one actor—and a neighbor of Michel Foucault's on Rutkowski Street—got grilled by the secret police on the circumstances of his frequent and hard-won rendezvous with soldiers. Further investigation revealed the actor was soldier-hunting not for espionage, but for perfectly innocent, sexual reasons. This sort of thing happened often. One professor, a friend of Zygmunt Mycielski's, found himself in a similar jam. According to secret police evidence, he not only was a "visualist," since his strongest attraction was to "sexual images," but also made his own films with soldiers and took erotic photos of them. These rendezvous made him a target for an operation at his home address that looked like something out of a Bond movie. His apartment was bugged, a few secret agents followed him all day and night, and his friends and students were peppered with questions.

The professor's predilections were well known enough to be reported in the press. One photograph published in a Warsaw daily was captioned: "In the above photo Prof. B. has donned a naval cap, as he is an honorary member of the Brotherhood of Friends of Seamen, as well as a Knight of the Order of the Pink Garter with Cocks Rampant."

Occasions

Lulla keeps her eye on occasions. Occasions are when you can perform and put on a show the likes of which the world has never seen. She marks them on her calendar: St. Andrew's Eve, Mardi Gras, the first day of spring, carnival, New Year's Eve, name days, and birthdays. These are when Lulla dolls herself up and goes out into the night.

Before the party: first, hair up in a headband. Earlier she'd have put on a mixture of beaten egg, sugar, shaving cream, and lotion. On her face: foundation, perhaps the brightening kind. Creams. Then a layer of powder—perhaps matte. Then her eyes: as she does these, she holds up her upper eyelids and bugs her eyes out. She adds colors and draws black lines. She applies eyelashes and darkens them with mascara. Rouge on her cheeks and some more powder. Powder everywhere: on her face, her neckline, her arms and legs—powder! Finally, her mouth. Red of course—what else? Then the wigs. Maybe long and curly, like Violetta Villas. Maybe a short, black bob, like Kalina Jędrusik. In a pinch, a cute little hat. Then clothes: stockings, dresses, stoles, feathers, opera gloves. And shoes: stilettos. Ready.

Lulla made into Lulla.

Lulla keeps her wardrobe in a shed out back that was formerly used by the building's residents for drying laundry. There she has all her creations hanging up in plastic covers. Gloves and other accessories are stored in drawers. Shoes on shelves. Lulla also has fabrics for her creations dating to the last century. She takes one out and shows me:

"Look at this gorgeous purchase! Double-sided georgette. A gem from behind the yellow-lace curtains!"

In photos from bygone years: Lulla in a gold sequined ball gown, long black lace gloves, a cigarette in a holder, high-heeled shoes, and blue eye shadow; Lulla in a black lace dress that stops above the knee; Lulla in a tight-fitting red dress and green gloves, with tinsel—probably from a Christmas tree—in her hair; Lulla in a purple dress with a shawl over her shoulders, gold accessories, and short, white, lace gloves; Lulla in a silver bodysuit with a white ruffle, black stockings and a gold wig; Lulla in a feathered ensemble . . .

The Amatorska

By day Lulla steps out in civilian clothes: green pants, a green top, brown leather sandals on her feet.

It's just noon, but the Amatorska is already full. A few tables, walls lined with mirrors—useful for observing the clientele. It's said the Amatorska's popularity was built on these mirrors. You could sit, your nose apparently buried in a newspaper, but with your eyes over the top of it, peering into the mirror and meeting other gazes.

Above all, everyone is equal at the Amatorska.

In the glass display case at the bar: a choice of cold pig's feet, tartare, and herring. Or sometimes only coffee—ground or instant too, or sometimes brought in a little bag from home; the waiters don't mind, they'll pour you some hot water.

The Amatorska existed in Foucault's day as well. Little has changed since, just that in winter there's now a smokers' booth by the entrance—back then you could smoke anywhere, but nowadays there's a special section.

Paweł Hertz could sometimes be found at the Amatorska, since he lived next door at 33 Nowy Świat. Here he would meet with his lover Władysław or wait for Zygmunt Mycielski. Hertz was very tall, very handsome, with classically beautiful and clearly Jewish features. He was talked about, people would try to go to bed with him, but he himself was not especially open about such matters.

Hertz loved the Amatorska, but he most enjoyed hosting tea parties at home. He would invite celebrities from Warsaw and abroad, especially Jerzy Zawieyski, Zygmunt Mycielski, and their respective lovers. They both knew Michel Foucault and it was one of them who'd introduced him to Hertz—but whether he and Hertz liked one another, we don't know.

Hertz and his partner Władysław lived close by, though not together. Yet they both had phones and often called one another—which we know because those phones were tapped. The transcripts of their conversations make it clear that by the time Foucault was living in Warsaw, Hertz and Władysław's relationship was no longer physical.

The secret police were interested in Hertz because of his connections to France and Israel. He was given the codename

"Pedant" and was surveilled intensively. The information the security services gathered on him was political in nature: "In 1958 Paweł Hertz was a member of a team intending to publish the opposition literary journal *Europa*. During this period he worked with the Crooked Wheel Club, where he gave talks on literature and art. He is a relative of a collaborator with the Paris-based [opposition journal] *Kultura*—Zygmunt Hertz, with whom he maintains active contact. Additionally, he is in touch with Konstanty Jeleński—a member of the International Association of Cultural Freedom and close collaborator of [*Kultura's* editor] Jerzy Giedroyc. [. . .] Paweł Hertz is a homosexual and from time to time hosts homosexual tea parties in his apartment. [. . .] Candid scenes from these 'tea parties' have been filmed."

Lulla tells stories about Hertz and others. She suddenly pouts and declares peevishly she doesn't recognize a single person here and the Amatorska isn't what it used to be.

"Nothing but out-of-towners."

And then she turns her whole body toward the sun.

She folds up her newspaper, finishes her coffee, and rinses her mouth with water.

She blossoms like a flower in spring.

An orchid, of a kind.

Colorful Birds

Lulla has hung the Dictaphone around her neck, leaving her hands free to gesture. She looks like an American traveler who's returned fifty years later to the city of her youth. All she's missing is a straw hat. She shields her eyes from the sun with her hand as we turn onto Chmielna Street. She takes a piece of paper with scribbles all over it out of her bag: she's jotted down important addresses and key locations, so she doesn't forget anything crucial.

"Chmielna Street, formerly known as Rutkowski, was like Warsaw's living room. Foucault would certainly have felt comfortable here—it was a henhouse full of colorful birds, of rising stars or long-since fallen ones, right in the city center, not too far, not too near. Perhaps the most significant of Warsaw's queer streets—and, though not as famous as Three Crosses Square, it did an excellent job serving its purpose. I'm not confabulating, I'm not colorizing. I'm telling you, authentically, how it was."

Tadeusz

At noon in his haberdashery, Tadeusz took some snuff for a pick-me-up. He gazed out the window, snorted some tobacco from his fingernail, and said to no one in particular:

"I am overcome with somnolence. I dream of boys."

The bell over the door was constantly tinkling. The street was crowded. His girlfriends from near and far kept dropping by. They'd taken buses to the corner of Nowy Świat and Foksal Street and headed for Rutkowski, but not for gloves or for wallets, but to visit their best girlfriend, the keeper of the city's secrets, "Madame Tadeuszowa," known to her friends as Tadzia.

People used to shout at Tadzia, calling her a parrot. She

would stroll elegantly along, looking straight ahead, never to the side, because why should she? She would smack her prominent lips: smack, smack, smack. She would sparkle with color like a kaleidoscope. She would put on a yellow jumpsuit, narrow at the hips, flaring out at the knees, topped with a pink blouse and a plum-colored jacket. Then she would pile on shawls, scarves, and stoles. And feathers! She adored feathers—hence the "parrot." On her head: a hat with a feather or ribbon, in her breast pocket: a feather or a handkerchief, on her feet: glistening little shoes with a feather and a low heel, sandals in summer, and in winter, knee-high boots.

"A lady from Paris," his neighbors would say in slight wonder, "except of course he's a fella, and only one from Chmielna Street."

Tadeusz ran a haberdashery, a fashionable boutique, small, but richly outfitted. Most important of all: *For men only.*

He was born in 1906 in Nowa Wieś, near Warsaw. In the capital he lived near the Polytechnic. Early every morning he would ride downtown. He'd unlock the door, turn on a small lamp on his countertop alongside the cash register, put the kettle on for tea, sprinkle a couple browning leaves of Ceylon into a cup, pour in the boiling water, and settle into an armchair behind the counter. He'd gaze out onto the street.

The first to look in was always "the Captivating Mrs. Cobbler," meaning Janusz, who owned a shoe store. Mrs. Cobbler was bringing Tadzia morning shoes trimmed with pink fur, which used to be fashionable and which Janusz had converted from ordinary flip-flops on the anvil at his store on Tamka Street. The shoes had a small wedge, because Tadzia liked to be a bit taller.

"Darling," said Mrs. Cobbler, "I come bearing new shoes of cosmopolitan beauty especially for you."

"Thank you, thank you, you're just in time," replied Tadzia, "because Sunday's coming, and I'd have been stuck like little Cinderella without her slippers, going to the park or somewhere with my tootsies bare."

And they chatted on like this. They dreamed of careers as stylists; of the wider world, which one day would see their greatness; of the streets of Paris, Berlin, and even New York; yet, ultimately content with their provincial lot, they would part ways in the afternoon, happy for the time spent together and full of hope for their next meeting. One would return to her cats on Polna Street, the other to her doctor husband on Barska.

Today the girlfriends remember that Tadzia's extravagance made her stand out against the gray background of Warsaw, but they never heard of her getting into any trouble because of it.

"The others were like little Chinese girls in uniforms, but Miss Tadeusz," says Lulla, "was like a bird of paradise, multihued, rainbow-colored, strutting proudly down Chmielna, because it was her home turf. Anyhow, all of Warsaw would come here like it was their living room, so what would you have had Miss Tadeusz do, flit about hither and yon? She had installed herself at the very center of everything and had it all right before her eyes. All the usual girls about town, and Mycielski, and that Foucault of yours too."

Other Possibilities

Foucault could go shopping for accessories at Tadzia's, or possibly at Moda Polska at 18 Świętokrzyska Street. He could drop his shirts off for washing and pressing at 1 Rutkowski Street #3—the site of Stanisław Baranowski's laundry since 1921, which advertised itself with the slogan: *Minimum time and maximum skill.*

If Foucault wasn't feeling well, he'd stop by number 6 to see Dr. Lasnowski, who got a lot of men out of trouble in those days. Two doors down was Zdrowie pharmacy, with service in several languages. Back then they sold marvelous drops, with ads proclaiming: *If you're tired, take drops.*[23] There Foucault could buy vitamins and medicines.

If he wished, he could go to Izis Cosmetic, Treatment & Cooperative. For wealthy Warsaw residents and tourists with plump wallets, this parlor offered dermatological, cosmetic, and plastic treatments, as well as gynecological and sexological advice. It was run by Dr. Helena Brzezińska. In 1960 there were twelve Izis beauty parlors, including two on Rutkowski Street.

The street appears frequently in secret police descriptions. Many people lived there and many came there, because there were places to see and things to do.

Mycielski

The composer Zygmunt Mycielski lived at 10 Rutkowski Street along with his partner Stanisław Kołodziejczyk. They were the founders of Warsaw's small cultural salon. Mycielski knew Ambassador Burin des Roziers very well, and met Michel Foucault at a reception at the French Embassy. Their conversation must have been sublime, because Mycielski was very eloquent and Foucault was interested in classical music. They exchanged addresses. Foucault wrote the directions down in his red notebook and remarked that they lived only a short distance away. They arranged to have tea, go to the Amatorska, and take a walk in Łazienki Park, then finally met up at the Kameralna, one of Foucault's favorite places to drop by.

Mycielski was friends with Iwaszkiewicz, and one of the ironclad items on the agenda for foreigners who were part of the community was a visit to the Iwaszkiewicz family estate. Foucault must have felt at home among this peculiar aristocratic company, made up of patricians, writers, and artists of various disciplines. Defert emphasized that Foucault made friends with people not merely because of their sexual orientation, but primarily with an eye to their level of cultural sophistication.

Mycielski was really a count. Naturally, neither his estate in Przeworsk nor his family connections could protect him from the People's Republic, and he spent his whole life depending on others' hospitality. That meant often traveling either to see his good friends in Sopot, or to Jarosław and Anna Iwaszkiewicz's in Stawisko, or finally to Paris. There he'd stay with Jeleński and his mistress, the Argentinian artist Leonor Fini, or with Giedroyc. The legendary composer and conductor Nadia Boulanger had also blessed him with her close friendship. Mycielski felt, as Hertz did, like an interesting but impoverished cousin from the East, because he had neither income from his estate nor a job, and no titles, leaving him only with an education from St. Hyacinth's High School in Kraków, one degree in philology, and finally another from the Conservatoire de Paris. He spoke French as fluently as Polish, which made Andrzejewski jealous. He had worldly manners.

The secret police gave him the codename "Turkeycock." He was described as "a homosexual, Catholic, and longstanding friend of Pope John Paul II."

Mycielski's closest friend was Paweł Hertz. When they couldn't meet in person, they would write to one another: letters, postcards, notes on napkins, or scraps of paper. They liked to gossip, about Jarosław, Jerzy, Henryk, but never about boys. This most important of subjects they left for face-to-face conversations. For instance, Mycielski wrote to Hertz: "I've had many visits, a few callers—but more about that in person," and set up a meeting for the evening, if they could manage it since "my dear, everything is lovely and beautiful, but I didn't want to say over the office phone that this evening W. is meant to come to my place. And it is certain to be a Saturday *intermezzo* amid the gray of the weekdays. [. . .] I would prefer speaking to you a hundred times over, rather than drinking vodka with Miss W., but what I'm getting at is it would be better to keep the two somewhat distinct. Therefore, thinking *improvisando* over this slip of paper [. . .] I will tell her we have important matters to discuss and suggest she make her way, by then a little vodka-ed up, to the municipal baths. If on top of all this our (very sweet at any rate) Miss Zb. swoops in on us, then I don't know, we'll entertain her as best we can."[24]

During their travels, they would constantly send one another letters and postcards. Most often from Paris and London, at least a few words or a significant picture: a naked boy by Rembrandt; from London, an obligatory soldier of the Royal Guard; from Paris, a view of the Café Bonaparte, a fashionable location for gay trysts also frequented by Foucault, Barthes, and Cocteau. They often wrote on hotel stationary, from the likes of the Hôtel de Paris in Monte Carlo. When the matter was urgent, even a napkin from the Kameralna would do, like the one on which Mycielski wrote nervously one Saturday to darling Paweł that he immediately needed the address of "that Dr. you went to. I need an urgent appointment with him—an unbearable rash and utterly dreadful symptoms."

For people like Mycielski, travel abroad was a way to gasp the fresh air of freedom, earn a little money, and stock up on essentials: shoelaces, hair pomade, shoes, socks, white shirts, handkerchiefs.

Diana

For all of them, the heart of Rutkowski Street was a sauna called the Diana.

The Diana was less popular than the luxurious Messalka on Krakowskie Przedmieście, but cheaper, homier, and easier to get to. It was located in a tenement building at number 13: from the street, you walked through the entranceway into the courtyard, then crossed diagonally to get to the door. There's still a ceramic sign by the old entrance in the courtyard, but that's all that's left of the Diana, because the building itself is now gone. The interior held a bath complex: you could use the city water supply just to wash, but not necessarily. One bonus was the bath attendant, who had a pack of caramels in his pocket for friendly customers—and for the needy ones, a kind word and a few złotys. Everything there was dependent on him, he turned a blind eye to some matters, and would also provide towels or the key to a locked room.

The Diana had charm.

"At the Diana, they burned real wood in a stove with iron doors," says Lulla. "That gave you a different heat than steam piped in from the heat-and-power plant."

It was also somewhat plain, furnished only with benches where you could undress, sit down, and remove your shoes and the lower part of your wardrobe. Then you would go downstairs, where life began.

In the Courtyard

One of the courtyards on Rutkowski Street, on the section near the Jabłkowski Brothers department store, was home to one of the most popular bathroom cruising spots in the City Center. There were plenty more, of course—many tenement courtyards had the same kind of little bathroom door tucked into a corner, which a person could enter to answer a call of nature. They were true communist-era temples of pleasure. You could never be sure, but hope sprang eternal. Besides, everyone knew imagination was better than reality. Sometimes all you needed was an atmosphere of airlessness, transgression, and some subsistence-level vulgarity. You closed your eyes and suddenly you were in Paris, London, Berlin. Out in the world.

"There were other points of interest in the courtyards too," says Lulla. "Mainly practical ones, because while you were out and about, a little shop might catch your eye, perhaps a glazier's or a cobbler's, or even express clothing repairs, done by hand for a couple złotys. If your button popped off, or a crease came undone, it was perfect. That's all gone now, vanished along with the latrines."

Another popular place to meet was the courtyard by the Hotel Terminus.

"Now it's called Residence St. Andrew's Palace, which sounds suitably refined. My, the apartments they've got there now, the suites! There used to be this Italian ice cream parlor in the garden, and now there's a reception, meaning security, though you can't see the doorman, so no telling if he's handsome. Terminus was a bad name anyway, so final, inauspicious. It's good thing in the end that Foucault didn't stay there. Which he might have, since it was cheaper than the Bristol, but just as discrete."

32 Rutkowski Street

"The street where the Atlantic Cinema stands," wrote the novelist Leopold Tyrmand, "lies at the very heart of Warsaw. [. . .] Approaching [its] western edge, the wanderer's gaze landed on the enormous skyscraper's cream-colored bulk and the immense, dusty space around it that trembled with labor: so without even stepping out onto Marszałkowska Street, the wanderer knew that another world began there [. . .], for this street, bursting with opticians, lingerie stores, and little soda fountains, was at the very heart of the great City Center district, home of government offices, banks, and businesses."[25]

The press raved about the broadened street and the apartment towers built at this very spot. The apartments were spacious, modern, aesthetically pleasing, and—as *Przekrój* reported—hygienic.

Before the war this was a commercial street mainly inhabited by paupers and small-time artisans. After the war, the name Chmielna was changed to Rutkowski in honor of a communist assassin executed in 1925. It returned to its initial name, literally "Hops Street," in 1990. The name refers to the hops gardens that grew all over this area from the eighteenth century onward.

But the street was home to another world, too.

Waldek shows me around Chmielna Street, opening that other world up to me. He points to the last building across from the Atlantic cinema. Address: 32 Rutkowski Street.

"It was here," he says, "these windows at the front. A tiny room, light and noise used to come in from the street. There was a sofa bed in the corner. And a desk. I don't remember any books."

Here, in apartment 27, lived Michel Foucault.

The building has since been renovated. A plaque hangs on the façade commemorating Dr. Jan Wyżykowski, an expert in copper ore. Not a word about Foucault, but why would there be? Who remembers that the great philosopher lived here?

Across the street is the Atlantic movie theater, and behind it, in the courtyard squeezed into the corner formed by two buildings, are double doors with protective netting over them. This was one of the busiest cruising bathrooms in Warsaw. Some fifteen years ago it was closed due to the murder of a boy who had only wanted to take a leak. The gay community assumed a little time would go by, the bathroom would get remodeled, and then it would be back in service again. But nothing has happened there since the murder.

"Sadly," say some.

"A shame," add others.

On the Terrace

A police booth used to stand on Bracka Street, where the two stretches of Rutkowski came together. This intersection was also a place to meet for coffee.

"There were two café terraces: the Świtezianka and the Niespodzianka. The girls would meet up at both to gossip and dish. No cruising went on, though, unless it was elegant cruises, because these were elegant places too, classy. Observation points are what they were. Right next door was the Cockerels, a restaurant where they served luxurious, saffron milk-cap mushrooms straight from the skillet. Milk-caps were all the rage in those days!"

Messalka

And on Krakowskie Przedmieście—the Central Baths.

"Messalka was a social salon. People spent hours and whole days there. You could come to the Diana, scout, score, and skedaddle. But Messalka was sophisticated. You'd emerge from the steam bath, hop into the pool, and then make your way to one of the massage rooms. There were these two rooms with stone tables where the masseur would lay you down, or sometimes girlfriends would lay each other down and one would massage the other. And the upstairs was elegant. The bath attendant, Tadzio, if he liked you or if you slipped him a few groszy, he'd bring you anything you wanted from the buffet, so you didn't have to come out half naked. You couldn't wish for much, but you could always get sauerkraut stew, beans and sausages, tripe. Some beer, and sometimes even a little vodka, if Tadzio hid it under his apron. And, well, Tadzio could see if you came to the sauna alone and then went upstairs with someone, and if you had a good rapport with him, then he'd unlock one of the private booths for you, with a cot and a little chair inside. Sheer luxury! And there you could, as they say, knock a couple drinks back and do as God intended."

In 1958, *Przekrój* wrote about the municipal baths. Only thirty percent of Poles had a bathroom in their house, though most didn't use them, because the bathrooms they had were often unfinished, so people turned them into storage rooms and pantries. It cost three to five złotys to take a bath in town, though hardly anyone had time for that. It was most crowded at the Central Baths, meaning Messalka (named after the actress and singer Lucyna Messal, who used to live above them—though her family prohibited her name's official use).

Messalka has long since closed, but its interior has survived, bearing the patina of age. The colored tiling is gone and paint and plaster flakes from the walls. Yet one beautiful mosaic in the shower room is nearly untouched, as is one small fountain in the shape of a lion's head, waiting to once again shower water on the naked bodies of the men of the city gathered here.

Cruising Spots

The cruising spots—where you'd go for a tryst.

"There was a place on Złota Street," says Lulla pensively, "which I think is active to this day. We often indulged ourselves there. Girlfriends would mince up and down, like they were on a catwalk or a promenade in Łazienki Park. They forgot it was an ordinary little street and they weren't headed for the Palace on the Water, just a local latrine. And once they'd picked up a gentleman, by hook or by crook, they'd slip through a gate, hole up in a little nook, or take the steps down to the john. A moment of rapture—and then instantly parting ways.

"In the '90s there was a copy shop here, but now there's another bathroom, opened up under the patronage of the 'Literary Circle of Coprophiliacs.' A poem of Tuwim's, if you please: 'All things depend on the ass.' And that's true. Down that way is a little coffee bar that's just like it used to be. It was called the Arlekin. It was particularly popular in winter, once the real cold started. You see, no one had their own apartment! You usually lived with your parents or were rooming with someone else. From the coffee bar you could pass through the courtyards back to Chmielna and conceivably slip off for another date, if after your chat you'd lost interest in the boy you'd picked up.

"This was how people met because there was no other way. No personals ads, those came later. Well, there were ads of course, but only on the walls of bathroom stalls. People would write all manner of things: poems, offers, places for hookups and the hours when they'd be there. No one had phones, don't be silly. It all worked perfectly fine, somehow. For instance, you might read in the bathroom at the Arlekin that, say, Mirek would be waiting on the corner of Francuska and Meksykańska at four o'clock on Thursdays. If you were curious, you'd stop by, maybe meet Mirek or maybe someone else entirely, who might himself have come to meet Mirek and had ended up not finding him. So now it's just the two of you, and before long you've forgotten all about Mirek and it probably won't be long before you've forgotten about one another too! Because it usually happened right away, on the street, in a courtyard entryway or, as I've been saying, in a bathroom.

"True democracy—anyone was allowed to step off the street into one of those latrines.

"The bathrooms were the clubs of that era."

The Bathrooms

There was nowhere to go, so you could go anywhere. For instance, to the Palace.

"The most gorgeous bathrooms, the height of luxury, were in the Palace of Culture," says Lulla. "Of course, there was a pool there too, but that was more for young people. For seasoned players, all you had to do was step off the street—on your way back from work or out to the movies—into the bathrooms at the Palace. Marble-paneled, with a separate attendant, who knew what was going on but never interfered, she just sat there quietly. Minded her own business, that's all. Everything smelled glorious, the tiles and terracotta scrubbed clean, really palatial surroundings. Unfortunately, someone tried to put a stop to all that and from then on you could only go in for a short time, after showing a ticket from one of the movie theaters, the Młoda Gwardia or the Przyjaźń, where the Kinoteka is today. So that was the end of chance encounters and cruising there."

Inside, Lulla lowers her voice as if we were in a church.

"The Palace bathrooms looked quite different from how they do now. First of all, there weren't so many doors, just open passages, entrances, and exits in all directions. Nowadays there's a tendency to hem you in, to block things off, but people used to want to go up to one another, to get close. There was a row of urinals against the wall, like the ones now at the National Stadium. Literally an entire wall of urinals, without any little panels or dividers, so you could see everything. You see, that right there is an important detail. It wasn't just queens cruising, it was out-of-towners and married men and soldiers, because you got no other opportunity for self-realization. Nowadays people complain there's nowhere to go, but look around, they've got choices beyond anyone's wildest dreams back then.

"I happen to think we were better off without the clubs, because what goes on nowadays is outrageous. They're discothèques, not places where you can go cruising. Well, you can a little, but it works completely differently. It used to be you could do it anywhere. Dance clubs and gay neighborhoods would never have crossed anyone's mind. Or these ghettos like the Marais in Paris, which used to be intriguing but nowadays you wouldn't touch with a ten-foot pole. You see, it's the same as ever: we're going backward and forward at the same time.

"The old stuff had a bit of flavor, you know, of savagery, but nowadays, where's the fun in grabbing someone's hand, pulling him into a stall, and getting down to business, then you shake yourself off like a goose getting out of the water and head home. That's not how we did it. For instance, you'd be walking down Marszałkowska, you had time, you'd see somebody you liked, you'd follow him or he'd follow you, you'd say hello, ask for a cigarette or the time, you wouldn't know if you'd have any luck or not. You'd start chatting, then it would all happen in a moment, bang! There was some risk in it all, some fantasy. Pure magic!"

Mushrooms

The public urinals are legendary. In Warsaw, the most important ones, the ones that formed the trail, were about ten in number. People called them "mushrooms" or "tin cans."

"Everything was blocked off from the outside. You could enter from either end, the left or the right, and the inside was divided into eight parts, like an orange. There were no stalls, you were pissing, pardon the expression, right there on the street. Some men would come in to piss and leave. But the ones who wanted to sneak a look at somebody, to score, they'd keep going in and out, circling around, going in again, peeking inside. This is how it worked: you pee, someone comes in, you look them over, you come out, someone asks you for a cigarette, a light, a match.

"The city knew about the mushrooms. One time a hooker went in. A lady hooker! The queens were in shock, everyone started shrieking, and she said calmly: pardon me, darling pederasts, I'm just here for a tinkle. Anyway, these were the mushrooms: the main one on Three Crosses Square, and then Zieleniecka Street, near Zamoyski Street, the Saxon Gardens, in the Behind the Iron Gate housing project, Grzybowski Square, Bankowy Square, the Eagle building, in front of Smyk's department store, on Puławska Street by Madaliński Street, and Rutkowski Street. You could always find somebody somewhere.

"Of course the cops used to poke their heads into the mushrooms too. But what could they do, I was answering a call of nature! No cop ever laid a finger on me, or hit me, or insulted me. And anyway, even in the clink you could have a grand old time! I once got held overnight at the station on Wilcza Street. We were in there with these call girls and we laughed, we cried, all of that. Because it was all us girls talking about men, and my, oh my, what a deep topic that is."

The Kameralna (16 Foksal Street)

"This was a delightful place and very fashionable. Foucault definitely came here, because it had the best class of customers, ones with good manners. But there were actually three Kameralnas: a bar for the cabbies, the nightclub, and the daytime bar. The night one had a dance club, on Foksal Street, where the Sabat Theater is now. Inside, you'd find Maria or Jadwiga standing behind the curved bar. They worked alternate shifts, Maria on even days, Jadwiga on odd days. The bar had snacks in glass cases: herring, pigs' feet, head cheese, toast with brains, phenomenal! You'd sit at the bar and Maria or Jadwiga would keep adding to your tab, writing on little slips of paper:

two vodkas, four vodkas, a half-liter of vodka—and take my word for it, Jadwiga liked to have a drop sometimes herself. You'd come in the morning for some breakfast and a vodka, then you'd head off to work or to run some errands and when you came back at two, Jadwiga would already be so sloshed that when she marked down whether you were ordering one vodka or two, you couldn't tell if she was writing in Cyrillic or Arabic. Both these gorgeous ladies adored the atmosphere at the bar. The doorman insisted on jackets and ties. At the daytime Kameralna, Zbyszek, or maybe someone else, would be in charge of the coatroom, and he'd always have four or five ties with elastic bands and a spare jacket. For ten złotys he'd lend you a set so you could get into the nightclub. The artistic program would start by midnight. Jurek sometimes performed songs. The room would be full of writers, actors—anybody who was anybody, the cream of Warsaw. Sometimes the fun would last until the wee hours, until dawn, until the next day. People would make their way home—to their place or someone else's—and not remember a thing."

The Kameralna was under nonstop observation. In the words of secret police operative "Karpiński," the café's customers did business there, shared interests, and wanted to get together over some vodka: "For the purposes of cataloguing the circle that drank at the Kameralna at this time, one must divide them up into the various groups that gathered and enjoyed themselves there. Doubtless those I name from one group knew persons from others and would often join up for shared entertainment." "Karpiński" goes on to list the types of female regulars at the Kameralna: the ones cheating on their husbands, the homelier ones who nonetheless got lucky, the ones who only wanted to drink without giving a thought to sex, and lastly, the ones who "found moments to take their minds off things, and enjoy life there." The men he mentions are mainly writers, painters, and designers, such as Jan Młodożeniec—"in this period a self-confessed alcoholic who, after six months of treatment, apparently no longer drinks. There was a period in 1956–1958 when he was regularly thrown out of the Kameralna by the coatroom attendants." Finally the agent added: "Over this period there were many regular Kameralna customers whom I got to know to varying degrees. Their leader was [Marek] Hłasko, a natural literary talent—he had a large amount of money, since his books had become very fashionable. Hanging around him were numerous drunks looking for 'easy prey.' These types were lost in vodka and had high opinions of themselves. Hłasko would buy a vodka for anyone who would listen to him."

The Kameralna was the most important spot in the city. Politicians would drink with actors, journalists with writers, careers were made, money was lost, fortunes were won. Everyone congregated there without regard to gender or sex—or, indeed, to skin color, since there was only one. As for colorful souls, there were too many to count.

The Kameralna declared it had: *Excellent cuisine—Superior service—First class band.* No wonder the crowds came.

"In a way it was a sort of sublimated, sort of rarified place," says Lulla, "but at the end of the day everyone was welcome there. For instance, there were hookers there too, of course. Both female and male, a wide selection. Though it wasn't entirely obvious at first, everything unfolded based on feel and good manners. As you were chatting, the appropriate sum would come up and you'd either accept or reject. No compulsion. Even so, the men with thicker wallets, they'd propose staggering sums you couldn't refuse. Usually someone would inquire politely: so how much for us to go and, pardon the expression, screw? Specifically the one carrying out this procedure would state an amount and you'd either make a deal or keep drinking, and that'd be that."

The Alhambra

The Alhambra café also had its own history. It was founded in 1956 and stood at 32 Jerozolimskie Avenue. Jerzy S. Majewski describes this cult spot in his book *Landmarks of People's Poland in Warsaw*: "The café décor was made up of variations on the theme of the Orient. The mood was set by wood panels, dark-red carpets, three lanterns, small tables with carved legs, and cushioned stools. Reportedly the designers sought inspiration in Turkish, Arab, and Moorish art in the collections of the University of Warsaw."

Some at the Alhambra were apparently excessively "flamboyant," though the place was particularly tolerant. Everyone knew about everyone.

"It was incredible!" says Lulla, excitedly. "Three big windows looking out on Jerozolimskie Avenue and a side entrance on the way into the courtyard, which is now walled-up. There's no trace left of the old Alhambra, there's a portal at the entrance and that's all. Now there's a bank where it used to be. Inside there was only one table, in the corner and behind a little railing, on a platform like a stage. That was where what you might call the head of personnel sat. She was someone who knew everyone and many people's fates depended on her. As you entered, she'd give a little wave from up there and welcome you. And then she'd cry out: ladies, where's the most fun place in Warsaw? And everyone would shout back: the Alhambra! Because the Alhambra had class, it had character. It meant something to go to the Alhambra. And being recognized in the Alhambra was like winning the lottery. You could get anything done by being recognized there. As far as behavior and proper manners were concerned, everything was allowed there and nothing was a faux pas. You just had to be human to one another. A simple principle. A Christian one.

"Since it was a café, you drank coffee. The décor and the atmosphere of the place were all reminiscent of Turkey. The drinks came in small copper pots placed in hot sand. So there was your Sahara. They poured real, aromatic coffee with foam. It had a unique flavor, a remarkable character, exotic and wonderful. Not like today, where you push a button and out spurts this coffee-flavored fluid—then milk or no, sugar or no. If someone were to reopen the Alhambra and return it to the city, they'd be doing a tremendous service to homosexual world history.

"The world's gotten so automated," sighs Lulla, "soon you won't need to fuck anyone in real life, you'll just hit a button and that'll be that."

The Roxana

There was also the Roxana at the corner of Krucza Street and Jerozolimskie Avenue. Large, curly neon letters spelled out the name of the club. Next door stood a police booth with a red button you'd push in case of emergency, though the booth wasn't actually manned. The button was rarely used.

The Roxana was an elegant terrace café. In spring you'd sit outside and watch Warsaw go by. The reigning queen was Karol Hanusz. He sat at his own table, greeted the city's citizens as they passed, waved and called over the few, in his eyes, worthy of making an acquaintance. Many people remember Hanusz at the Roxana like this.

"He'd share his table with people he knew or different ones who were just passing by," says Lulla. "Because Hanusz's style was that if he saw somebody intriguing walking down the street, he might curl his finger and wink: well now, my boy, would you care for a coffee, a beer? People used to say, 'grandma Hanusz is on the catwalk today.' He was one of the city's colorful characters, somebody who meant something."

Hanusz naturally had his secret police shadow. One agent wrote of the Queen of the Roxana: "An old stage actor, witty and amiable, who himself often makes light of his penchant for young men. If he comes across one of his type, he falls head over heels and always says: 'true love is always drenched in tears.' [. . .] At any rate he recounts without the slightest embarrassment how no young man can resist him, ages from 16–25. [. . .] [H]e doesn't like pederasts, only normal boys appeal to him, and the greater the womanizer the more he's attracted. He corrupts young men simply by having material means. He mentioned a certain Żorżyk from the Żerań car factory, he was buying four bottles of wine because he'd invited some boys over. [. . .] He is entirely alone. I have also heard of so-called pink Bacchanals, which take place in the artistic and literary community, apparently at these gatherings everyone has slept with everyone else."

The Melodia and the Sewer

"There was also the Melodia at 5 Nowy Świat," Lulla notes. "You'd find a higher class of life there. When, say, you couldn't get into the Kameralna—they didn't let everyone into the nightclub—you'd go along to the Melodia and if you were well connected, if you knew the doorman, you'd get in. They had a bartender who was adored and she loved all of us and loved getting drunk with us. Later on we discovered she'd been filing reports after every night shift at the Melodia and the Adria, where she worked as well. And that's why she was so nice at the bar, that's why our community trusted her, told her about our troubles, our romances, the people we knew—and there she was afterward, filing a meticulous report.

"But if you didn't get into the Melodia, there was one more wonderful, artistic club—the so-called Sewer on Trębacka Street, where the Kultura movie theater stands to this day. But not everyone could get in there either, someone had to bring you in or you had to have a good setup with the doorman, or if you had a membership card from the filmmakers' club then you could get in.

"None of these places were far from one another: the Alhambra, the Amatorska, the Roxana, and the Lajkonik—all within walking distance. And so girlfriends would flit back and forth like peacocks with their tails spread, to be seen at the very least, to join someone at a table, to have a word. That's what it was all about, being there.

"But there was life outside the clubs, too.

"For instance, on Ordynacka Street before the war there was the Staniewski Brothers' circus, which the Germans burned down during the war. There in a scorched little nook I had an incredible sexual fling fifty years ago. Someone picked me up. We didn't have anywhere to go, but there were these ruins and we, pardon the expression, went at it like rabbits right there in the ruins of the Staniewski circus. That's how it was done in those days, in the open air. In the elements. It never occurred to us it might bother anyone. At any rate, there weren't diseases circulating like the ones nowadays. To be sure, syphilis or gonorrhea were possibilities, but so what? You'd go to the doctor, get a couple shots in the ass and it would go away. But you wouldn't catch HIV, there were no AIDS carriers. It never crossed anyone's mind in those days."

Warsaw's Queer Mecca

And finally the legendary mushroom on Three Crosses Square.

"Which is to say," Lulla clarifies, "where it used to be, because our queer Mecca was vulgarly liquidated when capitalism arrived, and now instead of a mushroom we have a parking lot. And it's not even free! The first mushroom of the People's Republic stood next to where the little Chinese restaurant is today, which back then was a public bathroom. A bathroom is nothing like a mushroom. A bathroom means stalls and sitting there for ages to meet your physiological needs, it's an old attendant lady collecting the fee, it's toilet paper. But a mushroom is a different story. In a mushroom you could satisfy your aesthetic, romantic needs, or any of your higher needs, not these earthly ones. For if a person thinks sex is sinful or disgusting—even the bathroom kind, the ambiguous kind—then what can we do but pity them? Sex is and always should be the utmost delight. Who cares if it's in a bathroom? Or a park or a train station? On some bench? That adds spice."

We stand in the parking lot next to the Chinese restaurant as though it's a cemetery.

"If the mushroom was crowded, in a pinch you could use the mushroom-adjacent shrubs. You see here, and here—saplings grew, bushes, like in a park, it was lovely. And the square wasn't so well-lit back then. Besides, practically everyone knew what was really going on here. It was the city's open secret. But no one found it strange, no one made a fuss. People not only considered it normal, it was obvious and ordinary."

"Did Foucault come here?"

"You can be sure. There was gossip that sometime in April or May of 1959 he was seen on the steps of St. Alexander's Church, gazing hopefully toward the mushroom."

In May 1959, the weather was variable. Three Crosses Square was blossoming with magnolias—the white kobus variety, less popular than the pink kind.

The Antyczna and the Lajkonik

Three Crosses Square had, apart from the mushroom, two fashionable cafés: the Antyczna and the Lajkonik. The Antyczna was in the Griffin building, next to the Lajkonik, with a view of the mushroom. This is where Warsaw's bohemians enjoyed spending time: a few artists, a few gays, a few taxi drivers, and several policemen.

The Lajkonik took its name from the wall lamps shaped like the eponymous Kraków folk character, a Tatar riding a horse. In time, its walls grew covered with graffiti from its regulars. They were gorgeous ornaments, often evoking current events, full of irony. These priceless decorations did not last; they were destroyed in a renovation.

The Lajkonik was the city's information bureau for pressing gay topics. Anyone who was anyone would come by. Girlfriends would dish and guess how many people were visiting the mushroom. You could see the whole world through the window of the Lajkonik.

"Well that's how we lived, in full color, with one another 'ever this day at our side,' as the song goes."

"I thought that was from a prayer."

"Exactly!"

It's Zula, It's Zula

"I'll just add that what you might call my stage name comes from a prewar song. Do you know it? *It's Zula, it's Zula, a fur over her shoulder* . . . My friend Zbyszek, a.k.a. Maryla, remembered it wrong and christened me Lulla. My name before wasn't that different anyway—Luna, the moon woman, but Lulla is flirtier, lighter. Anyway, it was accepted, spread, and stuck. Lulla with two *l*'s, because I prefer it that way, I don't know why. Isn't it gorgeous?"

And perhaps nature, as a concrete form of the immediate,
had a power more fundamental still in the suppression of madness.
For it had the power of liberating man from his liberty.

History of Madness

FOUCAULT'S PASSPORT
(PARIS)

Collections

Daniel Defert was Michel Foucault's partner for over twenty
years, from about when the philosopher returned from Poland
until his death in 1984. In his will, Foucault left all his papers,
his works, archives, and unpublished texts to Defert.

Thirty thousand pages of archived materials were placed in
the Bibliothèque Nationale in Paris.

Foucault's private possessions remained in their shared
home.

Passport

Foucault's passport is a small booklet. Red, larger than a notebook, but smaller than half a standard piece of paper. It is not
an ordinary passport, but a diplomatic visa (number 913/58)

issued by the relevant government office in Stockholm on October 1, 1958. This little booklet tells us that Paul-Michel Foucault (in official documents he used the name on his birth certificate) "is authorized for a single entry and to remain in the territory of the Polish People's Republic for 90 (ninety) days from date of entry." Entry was permitted up till October 15, 1958, via any legally permitted border crossing.

Foucault reported to Warsaw police headquarters on October 14, 1958, and was given residence permit number 4927/2/58.

Foucault may have used his diplomatic passport a few other times. He definitely did when his father died (September 14, 1959). Michel traveled to Paris for the funeral. Probably also after he'd left Warsaw, but returned briefly to collect the remainder of his possessions. He surely traveled while in Poland, but we don't know exactly where or for how long.

Michel Foucault came to Poland for a second time in 1962, to deliver a paper at a conference. That was the official version. According to Daniel Defert he went, like Eugène Ionesco once did, to spend the złotys he'd previously earned. It was Ionesco who personally gave Foucault this advice. At the time, remuneration was paid exclusively in Polish currency, which nevertheless could not officially be taken out of the country. How, then, would he still have had złotys, when everything Foucault earned in Poland had to remain there when he left?

In his passport for Poland we can see only the black-and-white remains of shiny photographic paper and the slits in the page to insert the photo.

Daniel Defert is eighty years old. He has a gray beard, glasses in see-through frames, and his longish hair falls down the back of his neck. He is short, narrow in the shoulders and hips. He has slim legs and arms. He is not campy, though he nonetheless has something feminine about him. With his narrow fingers, he hands me various objects and always does so with grace (though without overdoing it). He shows me Foucault's passport and other keepsakes. He claims he knows little of him from the Warsaw period because that was before they met, and Foucault himself very rarely cast his memory back to Poland. Sometimes he would just say something in jest, and once or twice he mentioned Jurek.

We speak for over three hours. Daniel allows me to record, but not to take pictures.

Daniel

He is a sociologist and a philosopher, a social activist and a writer. He founded and runs the French organization AIDES, supporting people with AIDS.

Yet above all he is a witness to the life of Michel Foucault.

On the cover of a book-length interview, we see Daniel Defert's young face with light shining on it. In the foreground is Michel Foucault. The philosopher remains in shadow, but the photo gives the unmistakable impression that it is Foucault casting the light, bringing Defert's figure out of the darkness.

He has neither an e-mail address nor a cell phone. The only way to contact him is to write a letter, send it, and wait. His address can be found in the numerous biographical publications about Foucault. Defert replies to his letters by hand, in almost completely illegible handwriting.

Throughout our entire conversation, Defert does not refer to Michel Foucault by anything other than his last name. Meaning there is no Michel and Daniel, there is Foucault and his shadow.

"Yes, I lived in the shadow of Foucault," he says. "But it was the shadow of Foucault himself!"

An Encounter

After returning to Paris, Foucault settled at 59, rue Monge, and then—thanks to an inheritance from his father—at 13, rue du Docteur Finlay, on the border of the 7th and 15th arrondissements, near the Seine. He would often spend his evenings with Roland Barthes in Saint-Germain-des-Près. He would go out in late afternoon, though he liked the peace of his own home and writing; he oscillated between fun and work.

In the end, Foucault limited his meetings with Roland. He now much preferred spending time not in a sauna or café, but at home, with Daniel. He sat on the terrace and gazed at the city. He wrote and worked at a desk heaped with papers.

In May 1962 he became a professor of psychology at the University of Clermont-Ferrand. He spent his vacation the next year with Barthes in Tangier and Marrakech. While there, he learned the position of the Director of the Institut Français in Tokyo was waiting for him. A post he had once dreamed of.

He turned it down.

He preferred to remain with Daniel, who was just preparing to defend his dissertation (he was still a student).

Daniel stayed behind to finish his military service. Initially he was meant to go to Vietnam, but owing to the American war there, he left to spend his military service in Tunisia. Foucault often visited him. In Sidi Bou Said, they found their paradise.

Despite the topic of his dissertation, Foucault did not want to be a professor of psychology. He had always been closer to philosophy—so when he received an offer to lecture in philosophy in Tunisia, he jumped at the chance.

Every Friday afternoon in the Tunisian capital, hundreds of students and casual listeners would come to lectures in the largest hall in the philosophy department. Foucault had everything: fame, money, brilliant publications, an interesting job, a suitable partner, and a beautiful place to live. He and Daniel spent three years there. Foucault was overjoyed to be feeling genuine happiness for the first time in his life. Years later, he would say that in those days he was brown from the sun, fit from walking, slim from his diet, and more Greek from his love.

Life had finally gained meaning.

At the end of 1967, Burin des Roziers, then French ambassador in Rome, suggested Foucault take a position as a cultural advisor there. But now Foucault would never go back. He preferred research and writing to administration.

In September 1968, after the May revolution at the Sorbonne, he answered the call of Hélène Cixous—feminist critic and inventor of the concept of *écriture feminine*—and returned from his Tunisian paradise to Paris. His task was setting up an experimental university in Vincennes, outside Paris. In December he became professor of philosophy there, and Cixous founded the first Center for Women's Studies in

Europe. Foucault's course in Vincennes was on "sexuality and individualism."

Michel and Daniel decided to buy an apartment together. They had one requirement: enormous windows. They soon found a suitable place. A little out of the way, but quiet and, above all, bright. In fact one whole wall is made up of windows, looking out onto a spacious terrace. You can see the roofs of other buildings, but only if you look down.

Their home is on the top floor of an apartment tower on rue de Vaugirard in the 15th arrondissement and looks out on the sky.

Plenty of Sunlight

Foucault and Defert's local Metro line, number 12, is somewhat sketchy. Station: Vaugirard, with stairs going up and an exit straight onto a narrow sidewalk. On the other side of the city, this same metro line runs through Pigalle, home of the Moulin Rouge. But that kind of entertainment didn't interest Foucault.

If he took the train from here to the university in Vincennes, he'd have to transfer at Place de la Concorde onto line 1 and ride toward Château de Vincennes to the end of the line, and then walk for a good fifteen minutes. He could have also possibly switched from the Metro onto line A of the RER and gotten there directly. In any event it was a long trip. But it's very beautiful in Vincennes. It's a luxury neighborhood, currently one of the most fashionable and expensive.

The wall of the building on rue de Vaugirard bears a commemorative plaque, but—as on the wall of his Warsaw apartment—it's not for Foucault. Still, one is scheduled to go up soon. Apparently the building or neighborhood committee has finally talked Defert into it. The hope is the building's property values will increase. The fear is that it will set off pilgrimages of fans, and they'll have no peace.

The building has an interior patio, so noise from the street doesn't reach the apartments, and definitely not the one on the top floor.

In the apartment, a narrow hallway leads to the living room. The carpeting on the floor was once yellow, but is now the color of dirty oats. It's also full of holes, smaller and larger tears, revealing the gray lining underneath. The walls are similar—once bright and clean, now scuffed and covered in gray streaks.

Though the living room is very large, carved out of asymmetrical walls that jut into other rooms, it can't be seen from the front door. On the right as you come in is an alcove with a small table and two sagging, very uncomfortable armchairs. Against the wall stands a cupboard overflowing with papers, spoons for coffee or tea, saucers. There are loose papers, notepads, booklets, and books everywhere: on the floor, on the table and chairs, on the desk, which is visible from the door—traces of writing everywhere.

Foucault's workspace is surrounded on two sides by bookshelves. They hold first editions of his works, reading materials he consulted, books by his friends, titles published by Pléiade and Gallimard. Many are priceless. A few shelves, from floor to ceiling, with maybe a few hundred books—plenty, but not a huge number. Foucault didn't collect books. Nor did he particularly collect literature he needed for writing. He liked to do his research at the library.

His desk is gone now. In its place stands a modern piece of furniture: a large, black, simple table. The desk Foucault worked at was smaller, made of brown wood, with drawers on the right-hand side. On it stood a small radio and an ordinary desk lamp. Another lamp hung from the ceiling. To the left, a long-corded white rotary phone stood on a side table. Foucault would sit here in his favorite outfit: a patterned robe resembling a long dress, which covered his legs to the ankles and which he left undone, open wide around his bare neck. A cabinet was inserted into a small niche by the desk, its doors covered in bright orange fabric.

The cabinet is still there, but the material has lost its color, gone gray, with no trace left of the orange.

Nowhere is there any electronic equipment: no computer, no television, no cell phone.

The main eastern wall is an enormous window. And this window is the most important thing in the apartment. Now shaded by an orange awning, it still lets in an enormous amount of light, with specks of dust swirling in the rays.

We go out onto the terrace. Defert says:

"Now there's nothing here, but we used to have little tables and pots of cannabis. Foucault liked to smoke. But we finally talked him out of it. The neighbors weren't happy."

I imagine evenings on this terrace—summer in Paris. A few candles here and there, the smell of marijuana and the city air just beginning to thin. Down below, car horns are falling quiet, while the sounds of everyday life come from somewhere next door. The aroma of coffee, cigarettes, and weed. Foucault adjusts his glasses, runs a hand over his head, thinks. He smokes a joint and gazes out at the city. Daniel comes out of the apartment. He goes up to Michel, who is the shorter of the two, and they cuddle together with Daniel feeling his partner's fuzzy hair against his beard.

The phone rings. It's Barthes or Derrida. Foucault talks, one hand fiddling with the long phone cord, and Daniel sits in an armchair and reads. The large windows of the living room finally let in cool air and they can breathe, taking light drags of night air.

And of marijuana from the terrace.

A Photograph

Defert shows me a black-and-white photo. It was taken in 1973 in the apartment on rue de Vaugirard. Michel Foucault sits on the floor, wrapped in a dressing gown and looking like a praying mantis in a cocoon, or a geisha. He's wearing black socks and grasping his ankles. On his left wrist we can see a leather watch strap. The gown has come open somewhat, revealing his bare chest. Foucault's body is smooth—he's not only bald on his head, but on his torso as well. His face is clean-shaven. He's wearing metal-framed glasses—they look like television screens. He's squinting, his mouth open wide in laughter, revealing white, strong teeth. His laugh is either hysterical or theatrical. Foucault looks like he's posing.

Frozen in time, he is exactly as he should be: happy, loving, full of life.

The Little Red Notebook

Foucault's notebook is bound in red, coarse material. It's palm-sized, its spine is loose with age, but the yellowing pages are still in place. Information is written in three columns: *noms, téléphone, addresses*. Foucault filled up this notebook when he was living outside of France—in Sweden and Poland. Most people in here are French: Derrida, Barthes, Lacan. There are over a dozen Swedish names.

But only a few Polish ones.

Zawieyski

There is the playwright Jerzy Zawieyski, who labored until the day he died to reconcile his Catholicism with his left-wing views and his life as a gay artist.

Very talented, smart, rational, and creative.

Very ugly, closeted, anxious, and simultaneously an active pursuer of young men, especially at the Messalka baths, where he would spend entire days.

In his diary on October 26, 1958, Zawieyski writes: "Conversation with Zygmunt Skórzyński, who quoted for me the opinion of a certain French sociologist: in America there's an enormously developed methodology for sociological research, but there's a shortage of problems to investigate.

So they just take any old thing. In the Soviet Union there are serious and complex problems, yet no research methodology. In Poland there are serious problems and there's a rich sociological research methodology. Is that so? I was really pleased with this foreign scholar's opinion."[26] Zygmunt Skórzyński was on the board of the Crooked Wheel Club, a Warsaw intellectual organization whose most active period coincided with Michel Foucault's stay in Poland. The club's members included eminent historians, authors, critics, philosophers, political activists, and journalists, such as Władysław Bartoszewski, Paweł Hertz, Paweł Jasienica, Stefan Kisielewski, Leszek Kołakowski, Tadeusz Kotarbiński, Jacek Kuroń, and Adam Michnik. Foucault may have known some of these people. Skórzyński, as a sociologist, might have spoken with Foucault about his perception of academia in Poland, then conveyed that opinion to Zawieyski, who—intrigued by this young scholar from France—met him in person and struck up an acquaintance.

On the Avenue of Useless Meditations is Zawieyski's quasi-journal. It includes another interesting entry: "I borrowed from M. a book of Jean Genet's *Œuvres complètes*, from which I began reading the story 'Notre-Dame-des-Fleurs.' Initially, horror and the greatest amazement. But that's only the surface layer. Something else emerges from the depths. I do not hesitate to use this word: mysticism. Mysticism, which emerges from the abyss of vice, crime, and all sorts of evil. Fascinating reading, tragic torment, dread to the core of my soul."[27]

The entry is dated November 20, 1958. Michel Foucault was in Poland by then and only he could have had a collection of Genet's writings in the original.

Christof

The poet and scholar Krzysztof Jeżewski, who lived in Paris and knew Michel Foucault, gave him a present of an anthology of Polish poetry edited by the critic Konstanty Jeleński. On the first page is a dedication: *Reconnaissance, admiration, amitié,* and the signature *Christof.* Daniel Defert recalls Jeżewski was something like an intermediary between Witold Gombrowicz, Jeleński, and Foucault.

The Museum of Polish Literature in Warsaw has a letter by Foucault to Jeleński. In it, he writes about Hans Bellmer and subjects particularly dear to that artist's heart: the body, spiders, spots of truth, sadism, and the dazzling light of cruelty.

January 24, 1967

Dear Sir,

Enormous thanks for sending me the magnificent photo book by Bellmer. It is captivating. And of course, I was excited to read your article. In it you speak of the body, the inside of the body, the endlessly moving spider moving its limbs and grafting them, for an instant, onto their spot of truth. In it you speak of what sadism is and what it could be <u>today</u>, things which are doubtless among the most vital that I have read. And I would like to read much more of this from you. You have cast a shining light on the dimension of "simultaneous sensation," which is surely, doubtless, the space of cruelty.

I am deeply grateful to you for the moments I have spent reading your work. Please accept my expressions of friendship and admiration.

M. Foucault[28]

Rudolf

And then there was Rudolf.

Rudolf was a sort of gypsy, a traveler, never in one place too long, even if he wanted to be. He was from the mountains, he had the wind in his hair, a distant road in his eyes, but one eternal home in his heart. Still, he set off for France and settled in Paris. He met people. Was he outgoing? He could be if he had to, but at heart he was a loner. He would meet up with Roland Barthes in the Café de Flore, and with Michel Foucault in the Bonaparte. They both promised him a better life. They would say: stay, you'll get a scholarship, you'll do a PhD. He didn't. Paris was too beautiful.

He Was no Sly Fox

The Polish secret police had a very good opinion of Rudolf and had great plans for him. The young man was honest, intelligent, observant, and with a good knowledge of foreign languages. So they declared "establishing contact was intentional, owing to the possibility of stationing" Rudolf in France for an extended period as a spy.

He was selected as a candidate, vetted, and called upon to submit a report. An interview took place at police headquarters in May 1965. In the intelligence agency's view, Rudolf was not "some sly fox." Additionally he was skittish, which the agent interpreted as a typical characteristic of "his perversion."

The officer noted: "One important thing from an operational standpoint was that, without any pressure, he admitted his homosexuality and named homosexuals known to him in Poland and in France, simultaneously pointing out those with whom he had had more intimate relationships."

"You'll compile a report," the officer said to Rudolf.

"How?"

"You'll describe the homos you know. Especially gigolos and foreigners."

And Rudolf did what he was told.

Frenchmen

First and foremost there was Louis, a Concorde plane engineer, very valuable for the secret police. He invited Rudolf to the opera, the movies, to bars. He showed him Paris and introduced him to people. Rudolf thought he'd found love, but once he'd returned to Poland they only exchanged three letters "with emotional content" and then their correspondence broke off.

The secret police were unhappy, since after all an engineer is a significantly more valuable person than a university professor. And Rudolf only knew a measly two of those. An agent working with Rudolf wrote: "Sorbonne prof./philosopher

Michel Foucault, age abt. fifty-six, bachelor, after the war was cultural attaché in Poland. From conversations with Louis he knows he is homosexual, but they had no more intimate connection. Sorbonne prof./sociologist Roland Barthes, age abt. fifty, bachelor. Was supposed to arrange Rudolf a scholarship at the Law and Economics Faculty. Proposed him a joint trip to the Netherlands. From conversations with Louis he knows he is homosexual, though they had no more intimate relationship."

Maybe Rudolf made a mistake, or maybe the officer recording his confession got something mixed up—in any case at the time Foucault was thirty-seven and Barthes forty-eight. They would meet up in various places. Their favorite hangouts were Les Deux Magots, Le Fiacre ("this is an international bar for homosexuals") or Le Milord ("people from working-class and student backgrounds"). From time to time they'd travel to Chevrière—"an exclusive château where homosexuals gather."

From Rudolf's Reports

Rudolf filed his first report in 1965.

"I went abroad around July 5. [. . .] On precisely July 14 I arrived in Paris. [. . .] I got in touch with Louis Lepage. [. . .] Yet I did not meet with his friends, i.e. Michel Foucault, Roland Barthes. From Louis Lepage's account I learned that Prof. Michel Foucault was very surprised that I had come to France. Lepage said Foucault was convinced I would not come to France again. Additionally Mr. Lepage told me that Michel Foucault had great hopes to shortly accept the position of

Minister of National Education. This led him to turn down the position of *attaché culturel* [*sic*] at one of the French embassies in the West, and also to complain that he had to sort out the issue of cohabiting with his lover Daniel (I do not know his last name), who last year passed his final exam in philosophy, known as *L'Aggrégation*. He wanted to sort out this matter because he would be leading a public life in the future. [. . .]

"Louis Lepage [. . .] told me that his friend Prof. Roland Barthes is meant to come to Poland at the invitation of the Ministry of Culture (or Higher Education). He is to hold a sociology colloquium in Warsaw. Apparently Barthes asked him for my address, so I can guide him around Warsaw, and above all introduce him to a young Polish man."

In Warsaw

Rudolf kept traveling to France; he was studying in Warsaw and working as a tour guide at Almatur Travel Agency. This job gave him a fairly good salary. And since money stirs the imagination, Rudolf became popular in the Warsaw gay community.

"Rudolf had this funny little kink," recounts one of his friends from those days, "where he liked to pay some stud to lift him up and carry him from one side of Nowy Świat to the other. He got some unbelievable thrill out of it. The whole time he'd be laughing his head off and kicking his legs like a little kid."

Rudolf had one weakness. He was gullible and softhearted.

"You can't believe what people tell you," the secret police

major instructed Rudolf. "Don't feel sorry for these sorts of people!"

"But I'm not cut out for dirty work."

"Henryk"

They gave Rudolf the code name "Henryk."

"Henryk" had a range of plans, but the best fit was a project proposed to the secret police for approval: "enrolling in October 1967 at the Translation Institute of the University of Paris. Professor Barthes and Professor Foucault have promised to help me obtain a scholarship. If I do not receive a scholarship, I will begin work as a translator."

Nothing came of these plans.

At the end of 1967, "Henryk" submitted a written request to be released from his duties as a secret police collaborator. He based this decision on his nervous character, lack of "levelheadedness," and a fear that he would be unable to fulfill any of his assigned tasks. The authorities approved his request, their only condition being he could not leave Poland for the West.

In his last report, Major Gabrysiak wrote of Rudolf: "Intelligent, communicative in conversation. Freely discusses a range of topics. Avid reader. Well-informed about the political situation. Despite being self-sufficient and distant from his family for many years, he nonetheless has limited life experience. If a subject comes up in conversation that makes him uncomfortable, he blushes. Not always typified by confidence in his behavior. I believe this complex is a result of his sexual deviation."

The Library

Daniel Defert dispelled any hopes of a vast Foucault archive.

"There is nothing about Poland in Foucault's archive," he said. "Other than the short lecture he gave in Gdańsk."

Nothing was allowed into the reading room of the library at 5, rue Vivienne that could damage the documents, including pens or sharp tools. Laptops were permitted, but photography was not.

Foucault's Polish dossier at the library is a slim folder, tied up with cotton string and with a note tucked in the corner. The entirety of his lecture in Gdańsk comes out to six double-sided pages and is simply titled *Apollinaire*. Beneath that: *la mort d'Apollinaire*. The first paragraphs are written fairly legibly, then get worse, as if Foucault was hurried or bored.

In the text, Foucault emphasizes Apollinaire's Polish origins on his mother's side, which form the basis of Foucault's interpretation of the poet's work in the lecture.

Photographs

Foucault had two photographs of a young man he'd met in Warsaw. Daniel Defert showed them to me. One photo is candid, the other a passport photo.

In the first—Jurek is crouching in the city market square, feeding pigeons, hair blowing in the wind, his coat over his thighs and extending down to the pavement. He's wearing uncomfortably narrow leather shoes. He looks like a young James Dean—he has the same hairstyle as the American actor. The photo is in sepia. It shows knocked-down apartment houses, walls without windows, a few people in the background.

In the other photograph the boy is posing: face serious, hair brushed straight back, in a white striped shirt and a gray jacket. His wrinkled shirt collar and missing tie are notable, as are his dark, sad eyes. Jurek took this picture for his first passport. He was preparing to travel to France.

He was coming to see Foucault.

We must now interrogate the other side.
Not the consciousness of madness involved in the gestures of segregation,
with their unchanging rituals or their indeterminable critical debates,
but that consciousness of madness
that plays the game of division for its own ends,
the consciousness that describes the madman and unfolds madness.

History of Madness

JUREK

They Didn't Remember

Foucault knew Waldek, who had come back from America, sold two cars, and then drove a third like a maniac through the streets of Warsaw.

He knew Stefan, who wanted to stand on his own two feet.

He knew Mirek, who danced almost like an angel, but then married and settled down outside the city.

Later he also knew Henryk, whom people called "the Countess" entirely without reason, since he had no blue blood—just good manners and fluent French.

And Jerzy, whom the Countess promoted as an actor, but who only played understudies and replacements.

He also knew Zygmunt, Jarosław, Jerzy, and Paweł, who wrote various things, each one in his own way.

And also Rudolf, who lived in Paris, who was bowlegged, and who had a complicated history.

And finally Jurek, whom no one knows anything about, except that he existed.

None of them knew that they should remember. It never occurred to any of them that this was worth writing down, storing, safeguarding. Foucault slipped away. Peacefully, ordinarily, without fuss. Then, if someone asked—they'd be surprised, say it was a shame.

Little bits of hair on his head, glasses, a long coat, a checkered jacket. Apparently a sporty Jaguar. That's all they know.

Except that in Polish he knew how to say *pedał, dzień dobry, dziękuję*: faggot, hello, thank you.

That he would sit in the Bristol and write. Or maybe it was the Kameralna?

That he wanted to visit Tworki psychiatric hospital, but whether he finally went—no one knows.

Did he make it to the concentration camps or Kraków's Jewish district?

Did he see the Polish seashore?

Did he marvel at the city that had risen from the ruins?

If you asked them, they'd say: well, he was here. He was here and then he was gone.

Not much can be seen in the dark. Inside a mushroom no one looks one another in the eye. At the Tomb of the Unknown Soldier no one asks who you are, just how much you can pay. There was a bathhouse on Rutkowski Street, nothing more. There was nothing else on Rutkowski Street.

Except for him. In the apartment building across from the movie theater, in apartment number 27. If you went out onto the street, turned right and went a little further, the Palace was there too. Apart from that there's nothing worth remembering anymore.

Nothing much.

Nothing.

A Checkered Jacket

But there is someone who remembers him well.

"Michel was very elegant, refined," says Stefan confidently. "It impressed us that he was a *chargé d'affaires*, that he was French, plus he was chatty, kind, handsome. It was most often me, Henryk, and Jurek at Michel's place on Rutkowski. But Waldek definitely didn't know Foucault. They used to call him 'Walda Greengrass,' because she was always running off to the park, but Foucault wouldn't hang out with just anybody."

We're sitting in the Amatorska, drinking mineral water and talking about times lost to memory and about Michel Foucault, whom Stefan met by accident and whom he grew fond of on purpose.

Stefan, who was renowned for his masculinity, is still a well-built man. He speaks boldly, without fear of others or of nasty gossip, because he's never been flamboyant, so he can sleep soundly. He looks after himself and his partner. He lives a little in Warsaw and a little in Canada. He wears a large amount of gold on each hand, because it never loses its value. He has gray hair on his head and is clean-shaven, large, manly. Foucault's lover. His close friend.

Everything started with Henryk R.'s regular trips to the

French Embassy, to attend receptions held by Ambassador Burin des Roziers. That's likely where Henryk met Michel Foucault, whom he introduced to Jurek R. In time, Jurek became one of Foucault's confidants. They were very close, so close that he became the one Foucault would entrust with his apartment key. Jurek was fun, brave, helpful, and he knew many boys from around town—including Stefan, whose masculinity caught everyone's eye. One time, Foucault organized a little get-together at his apartment for his friends. Henryk brought Jurek, and Jurek brought Stefan. And that's how Stefan met Michel.

"I was playing second fiddle to Jurek, but Michel liked me, too. He was interested in the issue of homosexuality in Poland, whether for his research or himself, I don't know."

Stefan tells me he also had access to Foucault's apartment keys. Apart from that he didn't grow very close to Jurek and they didn't spend much time together on Rutkowski Street. Mirek was never there, and Waldek finally came over once or twice, but only when Foucault wasn't home. Everything Waldek knew about Foucault he heard from Stefan.

Waldek's story possibly arose from the need to ingratiate himself with the secret police agent, or maybe out of simple jealousy of Stefan. What he said comes not from his own experience, but secondhand. That's what Stefan says now.

"Michel was a wonderful, good, and friendly man," he says. "Anyone who really knew Michel wouldn't have informed on him for the secret police. Except out of fear, or by force, or necessity."

During his interrogation about the colonel's death, Stefan gave a statement about a few people, mainly widely known ones, but not a peep about Foucault.

"He helped us all as best he could. He didn't drink at all, not vodka, not wine, but he knew and understood that it was popular in our country, and so at his place you could always drink as much as you wanted and more. For instance, he'd get vodka from the grocery store on Krucza, because they had a store there for embassy employees. I liked and respected him a lot. And the sex was good, I have to admit."

Stefan explains none of this was prostitution, but true friendship that blossomed although it had no chance of going anywhere. That's how he remembers it today. He also remembers that whenever he needed money, he'd go to Foucault. Michel once pointed at a small vase standing on a table in the apartment, and said: Stivi, take as much as you want from here, whatever you like. Stefan tried not to take advantage of Michel's generosity, but he did sometimes make use of it. There were hard times, you had to be clever, finagle things from different sources, whatever you could manage.

Stefan knew how to live in the People's Republic. For instance, when cans of olive oil showed up at a store warehouse, the foreman called Stefan right away. They packed the cans into a cart and the young men ran to sell them on Szembek Square. Anything you could, anything that you didn't have but that suddenly appeared, could be sold. You'd be walking through the city and suddenly spot something in a store window: Italian bathroom tiles! You'd get right in touch with your friends, but quietly, so no one else got wind of it faster, and you'd scrape together a couple thousand złotys. You'd be in debt for a while afterward, of course, but to this day those tiles stylishly grace his bathroom wall. That's what foreign quality meant in the People's Republic.

Foucault's apartment was perfectly ordinary, with no luxuries. Two rooms—a living room, a bedroom—a kitchenette, a bathroom, a balcony. And that was it. Life there was colorful, because it was on its own terms, discreet, among friends. Happiness, joy, and a great deal of pleasure.

"Foucault actually did leave Warsaw from time to time. We had the keys and his place was free, so we'd throw parties. We'd play strip spin the bottle, and then we'd get together in couples or not in couples and hit the town. But he knew about it, he wasn't opposed. He accepted it and was glad we were doing it. Because he was generous. And he brought me back a beautiful checkered jacket," says Stefan, delighted. "Straight from Paris! Nobody had one like it. And matching shoes to go with it, a fantastic pink handkerchief for my breast pocket, pants with a crease—and when I went out in town, the girlfriends couldn't take their eyes off me. So I sold the jacket pretty quick, because I didn't like peacocking around, I'd always been raised to be modest and have good manners."

Besides the jacket, Foucault brought Stefan and the other boys pornography. They were pictures of naked men, single or in groups, a variety. The value of these photos was well beyond material—they were a breath of fresh air and freedom coming from the West, priceless. Stefan unfortunately no longer has any of the magazines from Foucault, but he distinctly remembers they caused a lot of laughter and a bit of anxiety.

"He brought back a huge amount of it, because being a consular employee he skipped customs. Pornography was illegal in Poland and so was prostitution, because there was this two-faced attitude! Call girls would stand on Poznańska Street, in galoshes, looking like they'd come straight from work, and everybody knew what for, and somehow it kept happening over and over again, sort of in the dark, except in the light of day. Those were the odd times we were living in."

Foucault liked Poles and Warsaw. He laughed a lot, never patronized, was always curious about new stories, never judged. He was very kind, a friendly companion. So why did he get treated the way he did? Nowadays Stefan thinks it may have had to do with his scholarly curiosity. He doesn't know what Foucault's thesis was on, but he suspects the Frenchman was researching "gay life here or the communist system" and therefore caused himself problems.

"He was always really curious about everything. Gossip from around town or political issues, didn't matter which. And that's why we thought he was, well, maybe not a spy, but just that sort of scholar by nature, nosy. But maybe also a spy?"

Yet he kept a little off to the side, he didn't get involved with political issues, didn't engage, didn't put himself at risk. He enjoyed going to official receptions, of course. But, as far as Stefan remembers, Foucault didn't really go to the gay clubs, or the sauna, or the mushrooms.

"Saunas were popular because people didn't have bathrooms in their homes. I went to the pool every day and I'd get a bar of gray soap from my trainer and every day that was my bath. But at Messalka's you'd get laborers and actors and soldiers and everybody. Never-ending crowds. It wasn't enjoyable at all, they let couples in and you could get away with something there, but it wasn't exactly fantastic or satisfying. Same with the mushrooms. The most important mushroom was at the Crosses, of course, which we called HQ. And lots of people would go, policemen too, supposedly to inspect, but there were other ways of scratching your itch as well. You'd head to the bushes by the deaf-mute school and nobody there would ever say no. But Foucault didn't do that, maybe he was afraid they'd recognize him, suss him out? He didn't put himself at risk, anyway."

Foucault had an apartment, so maybe he didn't need to.

One way or another, he had a different method of meeting boys: through chains of endearment. A chain of endearment means someone knew someone, introduced them to someone else, and then that someone else to a third someone, and finally this chain of endearment formed a social circle. This is how Foucault met new young men whom he took under his wing and into his cosmopolitan frame of mind.

Yet Stefan is convinced that this was all done out of friendship, it was platonic and non-sexual. If something happened it was because it developed as the two grew closer, not the other way around. Foucault didn't value sexual conquests, excesses, and easy scores, but intimacy. And conversation.

"I don't want to make anything up or misrepresent things here. He was different, but he liked sex too, make no bones about it. Like any normal guy—he liked sex."

If he went out, it would be to the Kameralna or the press club, maybe sometimes he'd drink a coffee at the Roxana with Karol Hanusz, from time to time maybe he stopped by the Lajkonik, but not with the Three Crosses mushroom in mind. On the other hand, he avoided the Amatorska—maybe it was out of his way, though it was right at the start of Nowy Świat, you couldn't miss it. You might stop by for a moment and end up chatting until closing time. The Amatorska was open from 6 A.M. until midnight and was full of life.

"People said Michel went off to Russia because he wanted to keep writing about the gays there. Then he came back to wrap up what he had here, but they pulled the rug out from under him and he didn't manage." Stefan only knows Foucault had to leave Poland, but he doesn't know why. He hasn't heard of any secret police sting, but he's not surprised, since such things have happened.

One day Foucault just disappeared.

"People said he was ordered out of Poland. I think people didn't like him writing about the topic he was interested in. He wasn't out chasing boys at all, they came to him, but we didn't know the secret police had laid a trap, because Foucault was plainly an upstanding person."

Lotus Flower

When he speaks of Foucault, he smiles broadly and it's visible how much this relationship meant to him.

"I had a special place in his heart. He literally saw a lotus flower inside me. He used to bring back photos, magazines, and different kinds of presents from France that we couldn't get in those days. Afterward, a huge amount got lost and it's a shame now. Whatever I asked him for, he gave me. For instance, there were these gorgeous shoes, patent leather and suede shoes—those I got."

They'd always meet on Rutkowski Street. Stefan knows other boys came there too, but to this day he's confident that his Michel was particularly friendly to him.

"I wasn't pushy or greedy. I wanted to earn everything myself and amount to something. Like a human being."

Stefan's apartment: a small kitchen, a hallway, room with a balcony as the living room. It's not that Stefan doesn't know about decorating, because his apartment in Canada—where he lives for part of the year—is simply stunning. But here he's got plastic mats with pictures of Niagara Falls on them, laid on a bench. On display in the wall unit are crystals and decorated plates with prints of Paris, for instance, or Toronto. By the window—a sofa, with Stefan's partner Andrzej sitting on it. They've been together nearly thirty years. The moment Stefan found out about AIDS he decided he wasn't going to die of it, and would stay loyal to one man, rather than potentially increase his risk through unfaithfulness or what you might call inconstant affections.

On the bench is a small vase of artificial flowers, a pitcher of homemade fruit juice from dinner, a mug of instant coffee, and a small plate with a slice of cheesecake. Stefan has many colorful stories to tell. He's experienced enough for several lifetimes. Two wives, two continents, three partners, loving parents, and a truly picture-perfect family.

"I remember when my aunt and uncle came to Warsaw to visit right after the war. God knows how much hunger and poverty we had here, and they were swimming in excess. My two girl cousins, all clean and tidy, dolled up, were too snooty to even sit down, they just kept saying to one another, 'good thing it's them serving the tea and not us.'"

And to this day Stefan says those words with bitterness.

More About the Boys

My conversation with Stefan keeps returning to Waldek. The two of them were together for five years, but when they broke up, Waldek couldn't accept it. His clinginess might have cost Stefan a relationship with Mirek—the dancer from the Mazowsze folk troupe. Though there were other reasons, too.

"He was a good guy, Mirek," says Stefan. "Affectionate, gorgeous, and talented—but anyway, when he got back from the Mazowsze tour of the States, he had ulcers all over his mouth. And that was the end of that."

In a photo from Stefan's collection, Mirek from Mazowsze has hair swept upward into a thick mop. Enormous eyes and a mouth that perhaps promises wonders. On the reverse side is a dedication to Stefan: of love and a lifetime together. Mirek loved Stefan so much that he even went to his parents and admitted everything. After that, Stefan's father had no other way out, he took his son to a café and said: you're grown up, you know what to do, just make sure people don't get a look at the inside label.

Meaning keep up appearances, don't let people gossip. No one wanted that.

"Everything sped up after that colonel got killed when 'the Weightlifter' bashed him with the siphon. It was all over the papers. There were two similar cases at the time: the colonel and Bohdan Piasecki, a boy who they murdered in a basement somewhere for political reasons. I spent a month in jail, they had dogs sniff me so they could supposedly recognize my underwear, then made me stand on sharp stones. It was a hell of a time!"

"And it wasn't Waldek who they tortured like that?"

"What do you mean, Waldek? Waldek went there of his own free will, why were they going to torture him?"

Stefan had been taking care of the colonel's dog, a Kerry blue terrier who looked just like a rag doll. The dog was too gentle to bark at the colonel's murderer. The colonel was gentle too, for that matter—he was writing an encyclopedia for the military, was a skilled linguist, and his only sin was loving young men and liking to brag about money.

For looking after his Kerry blue terrier, the colonel gave Stefan a shirt. The torture at police headquarters was a bonus.

Apparently once a person has been through hell, from then on, they're always prepared for it. Stefan's father taught him that; he'd been through it too and that was the wisdom he had for others. So this is why Stefan likes gold and is decorated in it from head to toe.

"When they find you, beat you, lock you up," he says, "take off some gold and buy yourself free. It worked during the war, it worked in communism, and it checks out in capitalism too. And besides, you can't get too attached to material goods. I'm not going to eat with two spoons, you know? Though in the end you've got to have something for a rainy day. Something durable, concrete, which will always have value and which, just in case, you can sell."

The Legend

Neither Stefan nor Waldek, nor any of the men I spoke to, knew the young man who was the catalyst for Foucault's eviction from Poland. Everyone knew there had been someone, but nothing more.

Foucault's official biographies and word-of-mouth information tell us his Polish lover was a student of French philology at the University of Warsaw. His "negative origins"—his father was supposedly a Home Army officer, loyal to the prewar government and executed by the Soviets at Katyń in 1940—meant he wasn't permitted to enroll in college. The secret police offered to make a deal with the young man. In exchange for the opportunity to go to school he'd have to become Michel Foucault's lover, inform on him, and take part in a plot to expel Foucault from Poland.

The many different sources offer contradictory information. But some points are always the same:

the young man was named Jurek,

later in life he married twice and had children,

he worked in a library or bookstore,

he was a public figure and it was important for some people to keep his identity concealed forever,

he visited Foucault in Paris,

he's no longer alive.

That is the local legend from Warsaw to Paris.

In addition, according to Foucault himself, he and his lover had a trap sprung on them at the Hotel Bristol. The police burst into the room and the only words he could make out were *pedał* and *kurwa*: "faggot" and "whore."

Evidently they didn't bother with *dzień dobry*.

Deportation

The cause for Foucault's expulsion from Poland was "immoral conduct." As shown by the example of Foucault's successor as director of the Center for French Culture in Warsaw, Pierre Arnaud, immoral conduct with women could go unpunished—but not with other men.

Poland was not unique in this respect.

A similar story befell Zygmunt Mycielski during his vacation in Paris in 1957. The writer Jerzy Kornacki makes ironic reference to this in his notes, titled *The Quarry*, which were confiscated by the secret police and today can be read in the library of the Museum of Polish Literature. On May 26, 1961, Kornacki wrote: "[. . .] today for lunch we have Janusz Odrowąż, who tells us all sorts of news from the parish, including a conversation overheard at the same table in the Bristol between [the author Stefan Kisielewski] and Mycielski. The latter laments that he has to use up every penny of his prize money from Monaco on paying off fines for pederastic hijinks in the public baths in Paris—he thought these were ordinary 'kids,' but they were undercover agents who locked him in chains and hauled him to La Santé, and only thanks to the efforts of Czapski and Giedroyc did he manage to go straight to the airport and escape, without paying the fine, but he's essentially banned from going to France until he pays it. As a result he's full of praise for Poland, especially Warsaw and its Saxon Gardens, where at any moment you can draft some military ass, especially of peasant descent, and you hardly have to convince them at all, and they go for cheap."

Mycielski mentions some trouble he got himself into in Paris in a fairly enigmatic diary entry dated October 21, 1958. The composer writes: "I was also nominated (or selected?) to be a member of the Polish delegation to the 10th UNESCO general conference in Paris. It happened, as usual, in a very seat-of-the-pants, last-minute way, and I was meant to fly two days later, led by Ambassador Wierbłowski, with Słonimski and some eight or nine Polish members to Paris on a 'diplomatic passport,' officially and with full ceremony. As far as my conviction under article 330 in Paris (a fifty thousand franc fine and a three-month suspended sentence), for which I had appealed through a lawyer for a presidential pardon (!)—I went straight to the new French ambassador, Mr. Burin des Roziers, and I asked him if I ought to accept this nomination, i.e.: would I get a visa for this diplomatic passport, which after all grants diplomatic immunity. Burin des Roziers received me very graciously, kindly, and warmly, and promised immediately to attend to the matter personally, requesting information from Paris via a courier who flew out that same day—and didn't rule out my receiving the visa. He therefore advised me to accept the delegation. So I went to the Ministry of Foreign Affairs and signed a request for a diplomatic visa. Yet two days later a messenger came to me with a letter from Burin des Roziers, asking me to see him immediately. I went directly, sensing bad news—and I learned from him, greatly embarrassed, that Paris had refused me the visa. We were now both pacing the room, with no pretense of gracious/ diplomatic conversation, he—clearly surprised, I—utterly 'up the creek,' not knowing how to pass off the refusal of my visa to the Polish authorities. Burin des Roziers returned my visa-less passport—and the application—*sans mention* that I hadn't received this visa, which is unheard of, so as to personally return the paperwork our Foreign Ministry had sent. He put me in a very difficult situation, which I decided to get out of by telling Wierbłowski the whole truth. Otherwise I might have been suspected of some collusion with the French Embassy. So I figured I was better off with that paragraph 330 (*atteinte public aux mœurs!*[29]). So I did that. Wierbłowski was at a loss. My going to the West on any official trip is 'up in smoke,' Burin des Roziers is an idiot to advise me in my present legal situation with the French to accept this delegation (which I could have refused, after all, pleading e.g., lack of time)! On top of it all, this ambassador invited me to dinner with the British ambassador, evidently wanting to emphasize his unhappiness with the decision in Paris. I thought of writing him back that—as *persona non grata*—I would not come. But I decided to go after all, despite not having a tuxedo or tails—just in what I had—in order to save face, since I couldn't save anything else."[30]

And Mycielski really did have his travel to the West cut off.

Did Ambassador Burin des Roziers draw on his experience from the "Foucault scandal" in resolving Mycielski's case?

It seems more as though he forgot about it, or didn't wish to remember.

Foucault's biographer gives this description of the situation: "Foucault had to leave Poland in a hurry. The story is rather muddled, but apparently quite commonplace in Eastern Europe. He met a boy, with whom he began to spend some happy hours in this gloomy, stifling country. But the young man was working for the police, who were trying to infiltrate

Western diplomatic services. One morning Burin des Roziers informed Foucault that he had to leave Poland. 'When?' asked Foucault. 'In the next twenty-four hours,' the ambassador replied."[31]

It was not so dramatic as that.

Daniel Defert claims Foucault always talked about the events with a fair dose of humor and sympathy for "this gloomy, stifling country," which in his eyes was nonetheless warmed by that "stubborn sun of liberty."

Stachura

If Jurek wanted to go to college, and the only route to do so was spying on Michel Foucault, then his name must be somewhere in the student registers. I broadened the period of time a little, since I didn't know when Foucault's lover would have theoretically begun his studies.

The registers of French philology students from 1957–1962 feature 130 names.

And only one Jurek. Or rather, since Jurek is a nickname, its full formal version: Jerzy.

Jerzy Stachura.

A famous last name in Poland. Except the famous Stachura—the poet—was named Edward.

And Edward studied French philology at the University of Warsaw.

It turns out the poet had changed his first name, and Jerzy Stachura *was* Edward Stachura.

Professor Henryk Chudak, a student of Michel Foucault's

and a friend of Stachura's, told me about both of them.

"Foucault was a charismatic speaker. The kind all of us lecturers would like to be. The hall was his, he was completely comfortable in it, like an actor on the stage. Without a doubt, he had an extraordinary gift. He delivered his lectures calmly. Little by little, he took authority over the hall and the audience."

Foucault was also eccentric, different, peculiar, and unforgettable.

"Meanwhile, Stachura was a vagabond type, always in jeans, a denim jacket, in sandals, without socks right from the start of spring. A little wild, a little on the sidelines, posing as Rimbaud. He was the only one allowed to smoke in Professor Żurawski's seminars. But I don't know of anything that would connect him with Foucault. Stachura was writing about Proust. Unfortunately his essay hasn't survived in the archives. There was a certain amount of gossip in the department, but nothing definite."

Stachura had difficulty getting into college in Warsaw. He'd come from Lublin and was only permitted to study at the University of Warsaw after Iwaszkiewicz intervened. During his university years he kept away from people, feared them; he had no money and was in conflict with his father. He contemplated suicide as well.

All of this is reminiscent of Foucault himself, who might have identified with this young Pole who couldn't find his place.

Was Edward Stachura Foucault's lover?

Professor Chudak looks through the student register. He stops at nearly every name and makes a small comment. She got married, she lives in Paris, he switched to the Spanish and Portuguese department. He was my friend, but he's passed away, she was a beautiful blonde . . . Chudak suspects no one, can say of no one that something particular connected them to Foucault.

I repeat the rumor that this young man apparently worked in the French department library. The professor considers for a moment.

"That's practically impossible. It was always exclusively women working in the library."

A few days later I check the French department library. A kind older lady shows me the room where Foucault worked, which today is an ordinary lecture room on the second floor of the building on Obożna Street. I look for Foucault's library cards. The librarian calls up older staff who might remember something. One thing is absolutely certain: no Jurek or any other man ever worked in the library. And definitely not Stachura, regardless of whether it was Jerzy or Edward.

All of this has been built on guesswork. Even the lack of a file on Foucault's lover would be fitting in this case. There are too many question marks. Hard evidence is necessary.

I'm building a ladder of suppositions and possibilities. Many of these things fit into a recognizable pattern. The image of a young and attractive Stachura as the lover of Michel Foucault seems likely. But there's no certainty.

I finally come across a convincing record from the secret police dossiers.

In one passport application, Stachura wrote he left for France for the first time in 1973. We know Foucault's lover visited him in Paris shortly after his deportation. Even if the story was distorted, a photograph of Jurek from this period should match the one Daniel Defert has.

But it doesn't.

Edward/Jerzy Stachura was not the Jurek from the legend of Foucault in Warsaw.

Truth Comes at the End

Daniel Defert showed me the picture of Jurek and the note in Michel Foucault's notebook with the young man's name and address. He also told me about how they met, the trip to Paris, how the arrest happened, and why Jurek did it.

I knew what he looked like.

I knew his last name.

I knew where he worked.

And how and where they met.

And then everything came together perfectly.

I confirmed Defert's information at the Institute of National Remembrance.

But the most important facts I established at the very place Jurek was working in 1959 when he met Foucault—the library of the Polish Academy of Sciences in the Staszic Palace. I made an appointment to visit.

And it was like the beginning all over again.

The clerk brought me the files. She laid them on a small table beside me and took out a form I needed to fill out. She additionally asked me to sign a declaration stating that, in the event of using information from the Academy, I would indicate this fact in publication.

She stapled the paperwork together. She wished a productive day and left.

And for the first time I held Jurek's file in my hands.

And I opened it.

Lover

Michel Foucault's lover was named Jerzy Tadeusz S.

He was born on July 24, 1934. His father was named Józef and his mother, Marianna.

In one of these documents, S. states that he was from a white-collar background, but this departed from the truth. His father's family came from the countryside, while his mother's family lived in Warsaw and were manual laborers. S.'s background could then be described as "peasant–worker," a phenomenon of the People's Republic.

Jurek's father was in the Home Army and participated in the Warsaw Uprising at the rank of a noncommissioned officer. After Warsaw surrendered, he was imprisoned in a POW camp in Germany. He didn't return to Poland until 1947. He died three years later.

Jurek's autobiographical statement includes his particular opinion on this subject. The young man wrote: "my father perished in 1950. My mother died in 1962." There is a distinct difference between "perished" and "died." Katyń was out of the question, but Jurek's father may really have been a thorn in the side of communism. If so, the young man's story about being unable to study because of his father and the necessity to collaborate with the secret police could have been true.

Jurek lived at 4 Sandomierska Street.

The same address found in Foucault's notebook.

Bookseller

Jurek was twenty-five when he met Michel Foucault. It was the spring of 1959. He had just earned a vocational certificate as a bookseller and was working in the Distribution Center for Scientific Publications at the Academic Library of the Polish Academy of Sciences in Staszic Palace. When he started working at the library, he was earning about one thousand złotys a month plus bonuses. Not much.

One day Foucault came to the Academy to visit the logician and ethicist Professor Tadeusz Kotarbiński. Maybe it was the professor himself who directed him to the library. Maybe he needed some materials for his thesis work, maybe he simply wanted to read the periodicals.

Daniel Defert remembers Michel telling him about the moment he met Jurek.

Foucault entered the room, looked around, and went up to the table where the young man was sitting.

He noted the shelves were sagging under the works of Marx and Engels. He asked why.

"Because no one reads them," replied the boy.

Foucault laughed and looked at the boy with curiosity.

"What's your name?"

"Jurek."

The Center for French Culture was located a few steps from Staszic Palace. Jurek and Michel could have seen one another as often as they liked—even during the day.

They could have coffee at the Bristol, a few hundred meters down the street.

They could finally, for greater comfort, book a room there.

Facts and Imagination

The Bristol was a luxury hotel. The hotel day lasted literally a whole day: from 6 P.M. one day to 6 P.M. the next. The hotel made life easier on many levels. Guests could leave their clothes and shoes to be cleaned, order tickets for exhibitions or concerts, and eat at the restaurant. The hotel would also book train or plane tickets for you. In some Orbis hotels there were even telefaxes. These services were provided for free. The Bristol in Warsaw was certainly the best hotel in the country (apart from the legendary Grand Hotel in Sopot). For a one-person room, Foucault paid about 100–150 złotys a night. At the time there were 227 rooms in total. The hotel was located at 42–44 Krakowskie Przedmieście, where it stands to this day. The phone number, now no longer in service, for the front desk was 6-32-41.

The Bristol housed luxury cafes and clubs. Leopold Tyrmand described one of them in *The Man with White Eyes*. If we switch out his characters for Foucault and Jurek, their story might have gone like this:

They stepped onto Krakowskie Przedmieście.

"Do we have to go into a café?" asked Jurek coldly.

"I think there's no avoiding it. I know one nearby that's empty at this time and cozy."

"Is there anywhere like that in the City Center?"

"There's one."

They crossed the street and Foucault stopped before the corner entrance to the Bristol on Karowa Street.

"At this hour," said Jurek, "we won't find a space upstairs."

"Oh, so you know all about it," said Foucault mischievously. "But I'm sure you don't know, Mr. S., that they've opened a new room here, downstairs."

They went into the lobby and then headed to the right, after taking a few steps down. A long, narrow room opened up before Jurek's eyes, with an enormous mirror with an ostentatiously gilded frame at the far end. Here stood two black, French-polished chairs and sofas upholstered in embossed, raspberry-red plush, and small tables topped with imitation marble. The walls were the color of milky coffee or tea, the ceiling with its motif of gilded fir-cones in a molded frieze was like something from the pavilions of the great international expositions at the end of the previous century; reinforcing this impression were the three chandeliers, seemingly made of gas lamps on gilded stands with pseudocrystal hangings around eight milky balls. Hanging on the walls were poetic illustrations by the famous Uniechowski.

"It's lovely here," said Jurek with a smile, sitting down on the raspberry cushions by the wall and playing with a metal champagne goblet holding napkins, "and relaxed . . ."

"I'm glad you like it," said Foucault. "Not everyone can

appreciate the soothing calm of this interior. Particularly not the young. But we mature people know its value."

In truth—the place was nearly empty and cozy. A few older gentlemen were chatting further inside, and sticks with newspapers protruded over a couple of the tables. Here and there could be seen faces in pince-nez glasses or the silvery coiffures of older ladies. At a neighboring table spread with magazines, someone sat completely shrouded by the pages of a copy of *Życie Warszawy* spread wide.

"What can I get you?" asked a pink and plump waitress, approaching in a white apron and cap.

"I'll have cheesecake, coffee, and a soda water," said Foucault. [. . .]

At the neighboring table the pages of *Życie Warszawy* quickly drooped. Yet not quickly enough to conceal from Jurek's sight a tiny hole, burned by a cigarette in the margin of the newspaper, right near the stick. A tiny little hole that an avid but nearsighted reader might carelessly burn, yet also sufficiently large to be able to precisely observe the nearest table and the people sitting at it.

"Splendid," said Foucault. "Do you see that man at the next table over? What a marvelous accessory of the café in which we sit." [. . .]

"Do you know him?"

"I met him yesterday afternoon. I have no idea who he is. Some sort of philatelist, I think."

"You're mistaken, that's not a philatelist."

"Well then, some sort of a collector."

"A collector. . . ?" said Jurek thoughtfully. "Of what?"

Foucault called the waitress. It was a cool March evening. A
blustery wind was coming off of the Vistula.[32]

High School and College

Initially Jurek studied at an international trade vocational high
school, and then in a bookselling vocational school, graduating
in May 1960.

He knew a few languages—German, Russian, and English.
There is no word of him speaking French. He knew English
well, since years later he worked in the Penguin bookshop in
London. He brought back a perfect recommendation letter:
"His knowledge of English is admired by us all and we're very
sorry he's leaving."

He never went to college.

In Paris

Jurek's passport application, which I found at the Institute of
National Remembrance, has the same photo attached as the
one Foucault had.

Jurek went to France only after graduating from vocational
school, a year after Michel left Warsaw, during the summer
vacation of 1960. He went three times—in July, August, and
September. This was the last time they saw one another.

Foucault welcomed him at the Gare du Nord. They got into
a taxi and drove to the apartment at 59, rue Monge. Along the
way, Jurek wanted to see the city.

As Daniel Defert tells me this story, he laughs and says Foucault also found it very funny that the young man was simultaneously terrified and thrilled.

They passed near the French Communist Party building. Glowing on the façade were the initials PCF.[33] Jurek couldn't believe it. He kept looking at the Party building, then at Foucault, then back at the building again.

"What is it?" asked Michel.

"Is that the Communist Party building?"

"Yes, of course. Why are you asking? Has something happened?"

"Does that mean the party isn't banned here?"

"Of course not," laughed Foucault. "It's part of the government."

Jurek burst into tears.

"They lied to me about everything! You see? Everything they told me was a lie!"

That was the moment Jurek told Michel the truth.

That he'd been hired by the secret police to spy on Foucault.

That he'd never been with a man before or worked for the intelligence services.

That even so he'd surrendered to the will of the secret police.

That their meeting in the library was not accidental.

That nothing had been accidental, because from then on he'd been informing, and this had allowed the secret police to stage the ambush at the Bristol.

That he didn't know at the time why it was important to them and had no inkling they were trying to force Foucault out of Poland.

Finally, Jurek even confessed that he came to Paris to write a report on intellectual circles in France, and Foucault himself was meant to be his bait.

He'd thought this was all for political purposes and was set up to support French communism, which the Polish authorities had claimed was restricted and persecuted. Only the name on the Party building made the scales fall from his eyes.

In Communist Poland, Jurek was a person with no chance of a career. After the operation at the Bristol the secret police gave him a choice: either they would destroy him, or he would work for them. College was put on a back burner, what counted was preserving his honor and his job.

He would have lost his honor, for being an informant for the secret police. And his job, for being the lover of another man.

Foucault heard Jurek out and offered to buy him dinner.

They spent the night together, as well as the few days the young man had in Paris. Finally Foucault took out a piece of paper and a pen, and wrote a report on himself. Then Jurek rewrote it all in Polish and delivered it to the secret police office in Warsaw.

The philosopher's report no longer exists. Daniel Defert does not know what his partner wrote in it.

Probably the truth: that he was an academic professor, that he lived in Paris and did not intend to emigrate to the Eastern Bloc, that he was homosexual, and that in his academic works he investigated the phenomena of madness, slavery, and exclusion.

At Headquarters

After returning to Poland, Jurek kept working at the Distribution Center for Scientific Publications at the Polish Academy of Sciences. Yet in December 1960, he received a job offer as a senior clerk at the Polish Armed Forces' General Headquarters research library.

He signed the declaration required to work for the military: that he would uphold professional confidentiality, that he is aware of the threat from "foreign intelligence services," that he would not be in contact with representatives of foreign governments or with persons living outside the borders of the Polish state without informing his unit's leadership.

We don't know why he did this. Perhaps they promised him he would finally be able to go to college. Maybe he was tempted by the salary? Or maybe he thought working for the military would be more interesting than in an ordinary library.

Yet two months later, Jurek handed in his resignation. He said his decision was based on a lack of appropriate preparation, a dislike of the long-term practices required by his position, and no longer wishing to go to college. "I cannot accept responsibilities that are beyond my ability to fulfill." His resignation was accepted on April 1, 1961.

He went back to working at the Academy of Sciences.

"Janusz"

We don't know why he once again got involved with the secret police.

It was 1978. Jurek was working at the International Book Fairs organization of the government-run company Ars Polona. He volunteered to become a secret collaborator and was given the codename "Janusz."

It appears the scheme with Foucault may have been an isolated case. After returning from France, despite his military job, Jurek did not want to be an agent. He was handling international trade for the book fairs organization, which was evidently considered valuable. He signed a collaboration agreement, but he didn't perform any assignments. He didn't inform. He didn't spy. He didn't take the secret police's orders. Finally, he decided to break off his cooperation with them.

The justification recorded by the secret police: the individual ceased to play a significant role.

Did he ever play a significant role?

People who knew Jurek claim he was a very kind and helpful person. "Clean as glass," said one woman who used to work with him.

Glass is easy to break.

Names from the Notebook

Michel Foucault's notebook contains the names of another several people whose identity cannot be established beyond a reasonable doubt.

At one point in the dossiers, secret police agent "Gustaw" jots a short note, including some names that line up with the ones in Foucault's notebook. The agent wrote that there were many homosexuals to be found in the Polish émigré community in Paris: "There are surely many more such contacts, and their clandestine nature could, after all, easily be exploited for more serious and equally clandestine purposes."

Another secret police collaborator reported on a postal clerk, J.—someone else from Foucault's notebook. The agent conducting the case added: "Since [the collaborator] himself is a member of that community, there is no doubt his statement is truthful." The collaborator who provided the information was codenamed "Janusz."

Questions

Why are there no records anywhere of the secret police operation against Foucault?

This is how it might have happened:

Michel Foucault was spied on. He met Jurek, who'd been put up to it by the secret police. They decided to meet at the Bristol for dinner, then Foucault invited the young man to his hotel room. The secret agents knew all this. Officers barged into the room and arrested both. The only basis could have been suspicion of prostitution. We do not know if Jurek knew he would be treated this way. Maybe this was used as yet another threat to pressure him into further collaboration?

Yet it is not clear why Foucault would have been so important as to have an agent follow him to Paris. Why wasn't it enough to get him out of the country?

Jurek earned little money, he might have accepted some from Foucault, although he probably wasn't gay and didn't date other men. Nor does it seem he actually did sex work, except in this instance.

Since Foucault had no valuable information for the intelligence services and Jurek was not a good agent, the case was closed and the paperwork was probably destroyed.

Probably.

For given that Foucault managed to return to Poland in 1962, we can bet there was still a file on him. Collaboration with foreign intelligence was the greatest crime in the eyes of the secret police and they would have noted his presence. Foucault would have still left a shadow in Poland. But there are no documents to say so.

Unless they still lie undiscovered somewhere, awaiting their moment.

Without a Trace

Jurek was a librarian at the Polish Academy of Sciences for fifteen years. He spent every day in a triangle between the Staszic Palace, the Center for French Culture, and the Hotel Bristol.

Maybe every day he remembered Michel Foucault.

Maybe he simply forgot about him.

Jurek's wife, Wisława, has since passed away. They had no children.

Jurek S., in turn, died on November 10, 2011.

Contact

In a passport application from 1961, in the section "contact with persons abroad," Jurek S. wrote only one.

Michel Foucault.

EPILOGUE: A WORD

The great, global gay revolution began in New York on Friday June 27, 1969. The police organized a raid on a small gay bar called the Stonewall in Greenwich Village. As usual, the aim was to write up a few queers or even arrest them, terrorize them, and maybe close the bar. Meanwhile, a few of these queers—flamboyant ones, effeminate ones, trans people, drag queens, some completely politically and culturally unengaged, not fitting the masculine standards either of ordinary gay men or the heteronormative world—said: enough.

This is how Gay Pride was born.

Five years later, in 1974, the first article on homosexuality appeared in the Polish press, in *Życie Literackie*.

In 1978, the openly gay American politician Harvey Milk called on American gay people to come out. He believed this was the only way to fight lies, myths, fears, and prejudices about the LGBTQ+ community.

At the end of that same year he was assassinated.

Sixteen years after Stonewall, in 1985, a surveillance operation on Polish homosexuals was launched under the code name "Hyacinth." These sorts of operations, which resembled a dragnet or a hunt, had been organized in the past, but never on this scale. To this day no one has been able to establish what happened to the thousands of files compiled during this time.

Polish gay people only started publicly coming out of the closet in the 1990s.

The years since then have seen:

the publication of the gay magazines *Inaczej* and *Filo* (1990);

the foundation of the illegal gay and lesbian organization, the Warsaw Gay Movement (1987), followed by the Lambda association (1989);

the first coming out of a major public figure, the author Izabela Filipiak (1998);

the opening of the first official gay club in Poland (1994)—Fantom, which closed in 2016;

the organization of Poland's first Pride March (2001);

the foundation of the Campaign Against Homophobia in the same year, chaired by Robert Biedroń, later mayor of Słupsk, political party leader, and presidential candidate;

the Campaign's most famous action, an exhibition of photos of same-sex couples titled *Let Them See Us*;

the introduction of a bill in parliament to legalize civil unions (2004)—since then rejected by administration after administration;

the magazine *Gala* named two men the most beautiful couple of the year: Tomasz Raczek and Marcin Szczygielski (2008)—a year later, as punishment, Polish state television did not broadcast the ceremony;

Euro Gay Pride took place in Warsaw in 2010, with around ten thousand people taking part—a year later, the parade in Rome gathered one million.

Some say the Stonewall revolution ended on June 26, 2015 when the Supreme Court of the United States voted to legalize same-sex marriage throughout the whole country. President Barack Obama, who had been pushing for the decision, said at the time:

"Gay rights are human rights."

...

Gay men came out of the closet to abandon the train station latrines, public urinals, and parks. To feel like part of the society that they had lived hidden in every day. So they didn't have to confine their identity to the night, to the basements, to the darkrooms.

So they could have a choice.

So that gay people were no longer a minority that could be and had to be hidden. Also so that gay people did not have to suffer in silence from the very beginning, without even understanding why.

Finally, so that no one would ever collect information on them, prepare files on them, look for dirt on them, blackmail them, and threaten them with consequences because of their sexuality.

To not be afraid, to be able to love, and to be themselves.

To be able to live ordinary lives.

...

The word that connects them all in their common experience of exclusion, which is their identity, essence, and truth,

which for many still remains a stigma, sin, or illness,

and for others a joke, a fad, or everyday life,

which allowed me to find the secret police files and became the foundation of this book,

which in the most obvious way defined this book's subjects and Michel Foucault,

as well as its author,

was:

Homosexuality.

ACKNOWLEDGEMENTS

I'd like to express my gratitude to the people and institutions that supported me in looking for traces of Michel Foucault in Poland.

They include: the Institute of National Remembrance, the Polish Academy of Sciences, the University of Warsaw, the Jagiellonian University, the University of Gdansk, the archives of the Auschwitz-Birkenau Museum and the Tworki Psychiatric Hospital, the Central Archives of Modern Records in Warsaw, the Archive of the Capital City of Warsaw, the Adam Mickiewicz Museum of Polish Literature in Warsaw, the Polish Writers' Association, the KARTA and NAC photography archives, the National Philharmonic, the French Embassy, the University of Warsaw Institute of Romance Studies, the French Cultural and Francophile Studies Center, the Institut Français in Warsaw, the archive of the Palace of Culture and Science, the Polish Press Agency, and the Bibliothèque Nationale de France in Paris.

I'd especially like to thank the people without whose help I would not have been able to collect this information. Thank you to: Ms. Agnieszka Krajewska and Mr. Michal Rosenberg from the IPN, the director of the Museum of Polish Literature Mr. Jaroslaw Klejnocki, the director of the Center for French Culture Mr. Paul Gradvohl, and Ms. Dorota Felman and Mr. Andrzej Titkow.

Thank you to all my interviewees for dedicating their time to me and granting me their trust. My conversations with you were always a challenge and a pleasure.

Thank you to Daniel Defert for meeting with me, and having a conversation full of longing.

To Michał Nogaś for encouraging me to work and offering literary support.

To Mariusz Szczygieł, for inspiration and the faith that this could succeed.

To Julianna Jonek, for editing and endurance.

To Justyna Tomska and Renata Mikołajczyk for your friendship and good (zen) energy.

My warmest thanks to my mom and sister.

And to Robert, for being there, and his goodness and support.

AUTHOR'S NOTE

The characters in this book are real people. Some of them knew Michel Foucault. They were often connected by acquaintance, friendship, and sex.

The places I talk about, especially forgotten gay trails, are often equally as important as the characters. They form the space of a theater stage and nothing would look the same without them.

In the case of the secret police agents, I list only their codenames.

Places

Saunas: Messalka (16 Krakowskie Przedmieście), Diana (13 Rutkowski/Chmielna Street).

Mushrooms (cruising spots): Three Crosses Square, Żelazna Brama Square, Grzybowski Square, Zielony (Dąbrowski) Square, Bankowy Square, the urinals at Wedel, the Eagle Building (1 Jasna Street), in front of Smyk department store, Zamoyski Street, Zieleniecka Avenue, Rutkowski Street.

Cafés: the Ali-Baba (the corner of Miodowa Street and Kozia Street), the Antyczna (18 Three Crosses Square), the Alhambra (32 Jerozolimskie Avenue), the Amatorska (21 Nowy Świat), the Roxana (Jerozolimskie Avenue at Bracka Street), Cinderella (16 Foksal Street).

The Hotel Bristol—according to legend, where Michel Foucault wrote his thesis and fell into the police trap.

Okęcie—the airport where Michel Foucault first met the boys.

The Polish Academy of Sciences—Jurek's place of work.

The Center for French Culture—Foucault's place of work.

BIBLIOGRAPHY

Michel Foucault

Foucault M., *Security, Territory, Population: Lectures at the Collège de France 1977–1978*, tr. G. Burchell, (ed.) M. Senellart, New York 2009

Foucault, M., *Mental Illness and Psychology*, tr. A.M. Sheridan-Smith, New York 2011

Foucault M., *Dits et écrits I. 1954–1975* [Spoken and Written I: 1954–1974], Paris 2012

Foucault M., *Dits et écrits II. 1976–1988* [Spoken and Written II: 1976–1988], Paris 2012

Foucault M., *Politics, Philosophy, Culture: Interviews and Other Writings 1977–1984*, New York 1988

Foucault M., *The History of Sexuality*, tr. R. Hurley, New York 1988

Foucault M., *History of Madness*, tr. J. Murphy and J. Khalfa, (ed.) J. Khalfa, New York 2009

Foucault M., *Histoire de la folie a l'âge classique* [History of Madness in the Classical Age], Paris 2013

Foucault M., *History of Madness*, tr. J. Murphy, J. Khalfa, New York 2006

Foucault M., *Kim pan jest, profesorze Foucault? Debaty, rozmowy, polemiki* [Who Are You, Professor Foucault? Debates, Conversations, Polemics], selection and tr. K.M. Jaksender, introduction B. Błesznowski, Kraków 2013

Foucault M., *The Order of Things: An Archaeology of the Human Sciences*, tr. Anonymous, New York 2002

Foucault M., *Discipline and Punish: The Birth of the Prison*, tr. A. Sheridan, New York 1995

Foucault M., *The Birth of the Clinic: An Archeology of Medical Perception*, tr. A.M. Sheridan-Smith, New York 1994

Foucault M., *Powiedziane, napisane. Szaleństwo i literatura* [Said, Written: Madness and Literature], tr. B. Banasiak, T. Komendant, M. Kwietniewska, A. Lewańska, M.P. Markowski, P. Pieniążek, selection and ed. T. Komendant, afterword M.P. Markowski, Warsaw 1999

Foucault M., *On the Government of the Living: Lectures at the Collège de France 1979–1980*, tr. G. Burchell, (ed.) M. Senellart, New York 2014

Foucault M., *Society Must Be Defended: Lectures at the Collège de France 1975–1976*, tr. D. Macey, (ed.) M. Bertani, A. Fontana, New York 2003

Other

Adamska U., Śliwicka A., *Szpital Psychiatryczny Tworki 1891–1991* [The Tworki Psychiatric Hospital 1891–1991], Warsaw 1989

Andrzejewski J., *Dziennik paryski* [Paris Diary], Warsaw 2003

Andrzejewski J., *Miazga* [Pulp], London 1981

Andrzejewski J., *Z dnia na dzień* [From One Day to the Next], Warsaw 1988

Andrzejewski J., Iwaszkiewicz J., *Listy* [Letters], Warsaw 1991

Barthes R., *A Lover's Discourse: Fragments*, tr. R. Howard, foreword W. Koestenbaum, New York 2010

Barthes R., *Incidents*, trans. T. Lavender Fagan, London 2010

Barthes R., *Œuvres complètes* [Complete Works], vol. 1 (1942–1961), (ed.) É. Marty, Paris 2002

Bartoszewski W., *Pisma wybrane 1958–1968* [Selected Writings 1958–1968], vol. 2, selection A.K. Kunert, Kraków 2007

Białoszewski M., *Tajny dziennik* [Secret Diary], Kraków 2012

Białoszewski M., *Utwory zebrane* [Collected Works], col. 1, Warsaw 1987

Bikont A., Szczęsna J., *Lawina i kamienie. Pisarze wobec komunizmu* [Avalanche and Stones: Writers in the Face of Communism], Warsaw 2006

Bilikiewicz T., *Klinika nerwic płciowych* [The Sexual Neurosis Clinic], Warsaw 1958

Buchowski M., *Buty Ikara. Biografia Edwarda Stachury* [Icharus' Shoes: A Biography of Edward Stachura], Warsaw 2014

Chomątowska B., *Pałac. Biografia intymna* [The Palace: An Intimate Biography], Kraków 2015

Cusset F., *French theory*, Paris 2003

Defert D., *Une vie politique* [A Political Life], Paris 2014

Deleuze G., *Foucault*, tr. S. Hand, foreword P. Bové, Minneapolis 1988

Dossier Michel Foucault, *Magazine Littéraire*, No. 435, October 2004

Eribon D., *Michel Foucault*, tr. B. Wing, Cambridge 1991

Eribon D., *Insult and the Making of the Gay Self*, tr. M. Lucey, Durham 2004

Gay Life & Culture: A World History, (ed.) R. Aldrich, New York 2006

Giedroyc J., Jeleński K.A., *Listy 1950–1987* [Letters 1950–1987], selection, editing and introduction W. Karpiński, Warsaw 1995

Guibert H., *To the Friend Who Did Not Save My Life*, tr. L. Coverdale, New York 1991

Gombrowicz W., *Diary*, tr. L. Vallee, New Haven 2012

Gombrowicz W., *Kronos* [Cronus], Kraków 2013

Grochowska M., *Jerzy Giedroyc. Do Polski ze snu* [Jerzy Giedroyc: To Poland From Sleep], Warsaw 2014

Grodzieńska S., *Kłania się PRL* [The People's Republic Sends its Regards], Michałów-Grabina 2008

Halperin D.M., *How To Be Gay*, London 2013

Halperin D.M., *Saint Foucault: Toward a Gay Hagiography*, Oxford 1995

Hertz P., *Domena polska* [The Polish Domain], Warsaw 1961

Hertz P., *Gra tego świata* [The Game of This World], Warsaw 1997

Hertz P., *Wieczory warszawskie* [Warsaw Evenings], Warsaw 1974

Hertz P., *Sedan* [Sedan], Warsaw 1948

Historia PRL [History of the Polish People's Republic], vols. 8 and 9 (1957–1960), (ed.) P. Juszczak, Warsaw 2009

Homo Warsaw. Przewodnik kulturalno-historyczny [Gay Warsaw: A Cultural and Historical Guide], Warsaw 2009

Iwaszkiewicz J., *Dzienniki 1956–1963* [Diaries: 1956–1963], ed. A. Papieska and R. Papieski, R. Romaniuk, introduction A. Gronczewski, Warsaw 2010

Jako dowód i wyraz przyjaźni. Reportaże o Pałacu Kultury [As Proof and Expression of Friendship: Reportage on the Palace of Culture], (ed.) M. Budzińska, M. Sznajderman, Wołowiec 2015

Jedlicki W., *Klub Krzywego Koła* [The Crooked Wheel Club], Warsaw 1989

Jeleński K.A., *Bellmer albo Anatomia Nieświadomości Fizycznej i Miłości* [Bellmer, or the Anatomy of the Physical Unconscious and Love], Gdańsk 2013

Jeleński K.A., *Chwile oderwane* [Interrupted Moments], Gdańsk 2010

Jesteśmy w Warszawie. Informator, przewodnik [We Are in Warsaw: Guide], Warsaw 1956

Kisielewski S., *Abecadło Kisiela* [Kisiel's A-B-C], Warsaw 1997

Kodeks karny i prawo o wykroczeniach [Penal Code and Criminal Law], Warsaw 1958

Komendant T., *Władze dyskursu. Michel Foucault w poszukiwaniu siebie* [The Authorities of Discourse: Michel Foucault in Search of Himself], Warsaw 1994

Kowalska A., *Dzienniki* [Journals], Warsaw 2008

Król A., *Rzeczy. Iwaszkiewicz intymnie* [Things: Iwaszkiewicz, Intimately], Warsaw 2015

Libera A., *Madame*, tr. by Agnieszka Kołakowska, New York 2000

Literatura na Świecie, Warsaw 1988, no. 6 (203)

Lemert C.L., Gillan G., *Michel Foucault: Social Theory as Transgression*, New York 1982

Macey D., *The Lives of Michel Foucault*, London 1994

Majewski J.S., *Landmarks of People's Poland in Warsaw: A Book of Walks*, Warsaw 2010

Miller J., *The Passion of Michel Foucault*, Cambridge 2000

Michnik A., Kouchner B., *Rozmowy w Awinionie* [Conversations in Avignon], interviews by J. Kurska, intro. by K. Modzelewski, Warsaw 2014

Musiał F., *Podręcznik bezpieki* [The Secret Police Handbook], Kraków 2015

Mycielski Z., *Dzienniki* [Journals], Warsaw 1999

Mycielski Z., *Post ludia. Artykuły, felietony, eseje* [Post Ludia: Articles, Columns Essays], Kraków 1977

Orgia z myślą francuską [Orgy with French Thought], (ed.) M. Falkowski, Warsaw 2013

Poland: Travel Guide, (ed.) Z. Uszyńska, Warsaw 1960

Prearo M., *Le moment politique de l'homosexualité. Mouvements, identités et communautés en France* [The Political Moment of Homosexuality: Movements, Identities and Communities], Lyon 2014

Pustoła-Kozłowska E., Pustoła J., *Hotel Bristol*, Warsaw 1985

Rachunek pamięci [Reckoning Memory], (ed.) W. Bieńkowski, H. Boguszewska, P. Jasienica, J. Kornacki, Warsaw 2012

Rakowski M.F., *Dzienniki polityczne 1958–1962* [Political Diaries 1958–1962], Warsaw 1998

Richter D.H., *The Critical Tradition: Classic texts and contemporary trends*, New York 2007

Rocznik literacki 1958–1960 [Literary Annals 1958–1960], Warsaw 1964, ed. Z. Gąsiorowska-Szmydtkowa.

Rokicki K., *Literaci. Relacje między literatami a władzami PRL w latach 1956–1970* [Men of Letters: Stories between men of letters and the authorities of the Polish People's Republic,

1956–1970], Warsaw 2011

Romaniuk R., *Inne życie. Biografia Jarosława Iwaszkiewicza* [A Life Apart: The Biography of Jarosław Iwaszkiewicz], vol. 1, Warsaw 2012

Samoyault T., *Roland Barthes. Biographie* [Roland Barthes: Biography], Paris 2015

Seidman S., *The Social Construction of Sexuality*, New York 2014

Seksualność człowieka w ujęciu wieloaspektowym [Human Sexuality in a Multifaceted Conception], (ed.) Z. Lew-Starowicz, Warsaw 2011

Selerowicz A., *Kryptonim „Hiacynt"* [Codename "Hyacinth"], Kraków 2015

Siedlecka J., *Obława. Losy pisarzy represjonowanych* [Manhunt: The Fates of Repressed Writers], Warsaw 2005

Sobolewski T., *Człowiek Miron* [Miron the Man], Kraków 2012

Sposób życia. Z Pawłem Hertzem rozmawia Barbara N. Łopieńska [A Way of Life: Paweł Hertz speaks to Barbara N. Łopieńska], Warsaw 1997

Stachura E., *Dzienniki* [Journals], (ed.) D. Pachocki, Warsaw 2011

Stachura E., *Dzieła zebrane* [Collected Works], Warsaw 1982

Tequila z Cortazarem. Kochałem wielkich tego świata – opowiada Marek Keller, marszand, aktor, tancerz, śpiewak „Mazowsza" w rozmowie z Dariuszem Wilczakiem [Tequila with Cortazar: I Loved the Great Men of This World – Stories from Marek Keller, art dealer, actor, dancer and singer in Mazowsze, in conversation with Dariusz Wilczak], Warsaw 2015

Tomasik K., *Gejerel. Mniejszości seksualne prl-u* [Gay-R-L:

Sexual Minorities of the Polish People's Republic], Warsaw 2012

Tomasik K., *Homo biografie* [Homo Biographies], Warsaw 2014

Tyrmand L., *Zły* [Evil], Warsaw 2011

Tyrmand L., *The Man With the White Eyes*, New York 1959

Un Institut dans la Ville. Instytut Francuski w Warszawie od 1925 do 1990 / L'Institut Français de Varsovie de 1925 a 1990 [An Institute in the City : The French Institute in Warsaw from 1925 to 19900, (ed.) Frybes M., Marciak D., Warsaw 2008

Urbanek M., *Waldorff. Ostatni baron Peerelu* [Waldorf: The Last Baron of the People's Republic], Warsaw 2008

Warsaw 1960, (ed.) E. Kupiecki, Warsaw 1960

Warszawa Białoszewska. Te leżenia, latania i transe . . . [Białoszewski's Warsaw: Lying around, flying and trances], Warsaw 2013

Warszawa. Informator [Warsaw: A Guide], Warsaw 1960

Warszawa. Osiągnięcia, perspektywy [Warsaw: Achievements, Perspectives], Warsaw 1961

Wokół teczek bezpieki. Zagadnienia metodologiczno-źródłoznaw-cze [Around the Secret Police Files: Methodological and Source Issues], (ed.) F. Musiał, Kraków 2015

Woods G., *Homintern: How gay culture liberated the Modern World*, London 2016

Veyne P., "Foucault Revolutionizes History" from *Writing History: Essay on Epistomology*, tr. M. Moore-Rinvolucri, Middletown 1984

Villiers N. de, *Opacity and the closet: Queer tacticts in Foucault, Barthes and Warhol*, Minnesota 2012

Zawieyski J., *Dzienniki* [Journals], Warsaw 2011

Zawieyski J., *Kartki z dziennika 1955–1969* [Journal Pages 1955-1969], Warsaw 1983

Zawieyski J., *W alei bezpożytecznych rozmyślań* [On the Avenues of Useless Meditations], Warsaw 1965

Institute of National Remembrance

IPN Bureau of Provision: 1268/10657; 01355/166 microfilm (MF); 1386/525693; 1005/83309; 2602/6538; 0201/265 vol. 1–2; 00231/172 vol. 1; 0204/1702; 0256/346; 01322/2881; 0246/988 vol. 1–2; 01322/1018; 1265/1053; 01224/1916; 0423/9743; 0192/773; 1535/70737; 728/6248; 003090/15 vol. 1, 10–12, 18; 001043/221 MF; 1633/930; 1532/2694 ; 0204/312; 0648/28 vol. 2; 0785/5; 0296/172 vol. 1–2; 0296/171 vol. 23; 01322/1018; 01322/2881; 0423/7822; 003090/15 vol. 2–9, 13–17, 19–26; 01569/19/DVD; 01322/1018; 728/51364; 001121/752 MF; 00249/163 vol. 1–4; 01262/717 MF; 001043/2196 MF; 00191/154; 910/1681; 1001/58568; 728/40191; 728/25218; 728/26702; 1001/26227; 728/15612; 0423/7826/CD; 003189/6; 01222/1633; 0423/7822; 0999/34 vol. 16; 1368/11606; 0423/7820; 0326/128; 728/75605; 002082/227; 0248/207; 01434/279; 002082/78; 1559/101; 1386/16682; 001101/2061 MF; 002086/ 540 MF; 01434/383 MF; 001102/2113 MF; 01975/1122 MF; 001102/2068 MF; 01434/296 MF; 001043/1389 MF; 01137/97; 002086/1637 MF; 002086/256 MF; 01168/403 MF; 01299/73; 01299/550; 00231/195 vol. 1; 01062/27 vol. 2; 01967/104 MF; 01967/30 MF; 0604/22; 0951/689; 728/46390; 49 vol. 1–2; 01419/198; 0236/175 vol. 1–3; 0296/248 vol. 1–5; 0204/503 vol. 1–9;

01419/352 MF; 0449/26 vol. 30; 003371/1; 01911/40; 01940/63; 1098/14 vol. 656; 1585/23334; 001043/2278 MF; 00191/173; 0332/224 vol. 1–2; 00945/2606 MF; 01434/388 MF; 00945/2606 MF; 01434/388 MF; 0236/142 vol. 1–4; 0423/7822; 0203/1392; 1386/520030; 763/21970; 1010/502; 0330/292 vol. 3; 1423/5626; 00945/327 MF; 001043/687 MF; 00170/721; 001102/1977 MF; 2198/5502; 0604/32; 2386/15126; 763/88313; 728/55818; 01434/279; 01285/312; 1510/4002; 1510/1308; 1510/2043; 01299/127; 0204/312; 0224/111; 0224/458; 01334/649; 0236/142 vol. 1–4; 2739/1; 1585/21866; 01820/15 vol. 146; 0332/222 vol. 1–11; 001043/588; 01224/315; 01228/941; 0222/551; 0423/7818; 0423/7824; 01264/466; 01224/434; 0236/175 vol. 1–3; 01419/198; 0423/7821; 001043/2499 MF; 01224/434; 01178/289; 0365/111 vol. 3; 763/78253; 01325/29/J; 01220/10 vol. 202; 0332/222 vol. 1–11; 1585/1115; 00945/372; 01224/292; 01178/289; 0604/32; 01220/10 vol. 202; 0423/7821; 01224/247; 01178/289; Main Commission: 366/1217; 193/104; 164/1712; 164/2453; 131/23; 825/7; Lustration Bureau: 360/26525; 00419/797; Inventory Bureau: 404/249 (Formerly: Main Commission 230/249);
+ Copies of 49 registration records pages;

Archive of the Museum of Polish Literature

1713; 1714; 1715; 1547; 1554; 1576; 1586; 1587; 1600

ENDNOTES

[1] T. Bilikiewicz, *Klinika nerwic płciowych* [Clinic of Sexual Neuroses], Warsaw, 1958, p. 98.

[2] Should be: *Si le grain ne meurt* [If It Die] by André Gide

[3] Should be: *Man is Naked* by Grzegorz Timofiejew

[4] Should be: *The Gates of Paradise* by Jerzy Andrzejewski

[5] The agent preparing this memorandum made a mistake. Michel Foucault lived at 32 Rutkowski Street.

[6] J. Kalkowski, "Ile wart jest dolar?" [How much is a dollar worth?], *Przekrój* no. 707 (October 26, 1958), p. 17.

[7] H. Krall, "Pałac [The Palace]" in *Jako dowód i wyraz przyjaźni. Reportaże o Pałacu Kultury* [As Proof and Expression of Friendship: Reportage on the Palace of Culture], ed. M. Budzinska, M. Sznajderman, Wołowiec 2015, p. 206

[8] See: *Un Institut dans la ville*, Warsaw 2008

[9] É. Burin des Roziers, "Une rencontre à Varsovie [A Meeting in Warsaw]," *Le Debat* no. 41, September–November 1986, p. 133, quoted in D. Eribon, *Michel Foucault*, tr. Betsy Wing, Cambridge 1991, p. 87

[10] Ibid., p. 88

[11] "Pokaz filmu Cocteau" [Screening of Cocteau Film], *Życie Warszawy*, no. 254, October 23–24, 1960, p. 2

[12] Françoise played Marguerite in Janusz Morgenstern's film *Goodbye, See you Tomorrow.*

[13] *Histoire de la folie à l'âge classique*, Paris 1972; *History of Madness*, tr. J. Murphy, J. Khalifa, London-New York 2009. I give both editions because the foreword I mention above was only reprinted in the full English edition (p. xxxv). Current editions of *History of Madness* usually only provide the 1972 foreword, in which the words "stubborn sun of Polish liberty" do not appear.

[14] M. Foucault, "Lettre à un ami" (November 22, 1958), in M. Foucault, *Dits et ecrits I. 1954–1975*, Paris 2001, p. 27.

[15] Ibid.

[16] M. Foucault, op. cit., 2009, p. xxxvi

[17] D. Eribon, op. cit., p. 89

[18] M. Foucault, *Herculine Barbin dite Alexina B.*, Paris 1978.

[19] D. Eribon, op. cit., p. 299

[20] See D. Macy, *The Lives of Michel Foucault*, London 1993

[21] Eribon, op. cit., p. 327

[22] Ibid., p. 328

[23] *If you're tired, if you're going to make an exhausting trip, if the weather is too hot, if the weather is too foul—take DROPS (Mint, Fruit, Vitamin, Coffee). They refresh your breath, they disinfect your respiratory organs, they strengthen your heart, they stimulate your nervous system.*

[24] Quote from manuscript of letter from Zygmunt Mycielski to Paweł Hertz (Museum of Polish Literature).

[25] L. Tyrmand, *Zły* [Evil], Kraków 2011, p. 243, this excerpt translated by Sean Gasper Bye. *Zły* was published in abridged form in English under the title *The Man with the White Eyes*, tr. David Welsh, New York 1959.

[26] J. Zawieyski, *Dzienniki* [Diaries], vol. I, Warsaw 2011, p. 601.

[27] J. Zawieyski, *W alei bezpożytecznych rozmyślań* [On the Avenue of Useless Meditations], Warsaw, 1965, pp. 96–96. Exactly one year later, Zawieyski also mentioned Jean Bourilly, Foucault's successor in Warsaw.

[28] K.A. Jeleński, *Chwile oderwane* [Unconnected Moments], ed. P. Kłoczowski, Gdańsk 2010, p. 560. A photograph of Foucault's original letter is found in the same book on pp. 147–148.

[29] Public indecency (French).

[30] Z. Mycielski, *Dziennik 1950–1959* [Journal 1950–1959], Warsaw 1999, pp. 360–361.

[31] D. Eribon, op. cit., p. 89.

[32] Adapted from L. Tyrmand, op. cit., pp. 79–84. Excerpt translated by Sean Gasper Bye.

[33] *Parti communiste français*, i.e. French Communist Party

Remigiusz Ryziński is a professor of philosophy, writer, translator, and theorist of feminism and masculinity studies. His book *Foucault in Warsaw* was nominated for the Nike, Poland's most prestigious literary award. His second book of reportage, *A Stranger Story*, was published in 2018. His latest book, *My Life Is My Own: Stories of Freedom and Desire* was a surprise hit, selling out its print run in six days, and a stage version premiered in November 2020. Ryziński was named Public Figure of the Year at the Natwest LGBT+ Diamonds awards in 2018. He sits on the Academic Council of the Center for Social Research on Sexuality at the University of Warsaw.

Sean Gasper Bye is a translator of Polish fiction, reportage, and drama. He has published translations of *Watercolours* by Lidia Ostałowska, *History of a Disappearance* by Filip Springer, *The King of Warsaw* by Szczepan Twardoch, and *Ellis Island: A People's History* by Małgorzata Szejnert. He is a winner of the 2016 Asymptote Close Approximations Prize, a 2019 National Endowment for the Arts translation fellow, and former Literature and Humanities Curator at the Polish Cultural Institute New York.